TIME ON OUR HANDS

Other Books by Ron Cook

Charles Blue Paranormal Mysteries

Firebrand #1
The Last Family of Wizards #2
Time on Our Hands #3

On Guard in the General's Chorus:
Army & Korea Stories 1966-1968

Onward Through the Fog: Short Stories & Mystery
Novelettes

A Young Upstart: Poetry & Contour Drawings 1977-1982

The Mountain Dulcimer

Time on Our Hands

A Charles Blue Paranormal Mystery #3

Ron Cook

Time on Our Hands

For Charlie
Sixty years of friendship and adventures

Prologue

East Anglia, 7th Century

The cold, damp ground made it hard for us to sleep. Two days ago, we arrived in Anglialand after a storm-tossed three-day voyage from our Noreg homeland. The weather here in Sutton Hoo seemed so much wetter than our own. Our layers of woolen clothes protected us in the snow back home but held the dampness of the cold rain of this region. Even our reindeer-skin boots could not keep the water off our feet. We rose shivering and stoked the stubborn fires before first light.

We arrived here to attack the fortress of Malcolm the Cruel. It was he and his army who had raided, killed, and destroyed one of our villages last year. We came to return the favor. However, struggling to row up the flooded river, we ran aground in the changing current. Our vessel became bogged down in the soft mud. It seemed that the recent heavy rains washed most of Anglialand downriver, and the mud was building up around our ship's hull as its weight made it sink deeper into the mire. No gods or the spells of our shaman could help us now.

As the sun came up, three warriors, including myself, went in search of fresh meat. Yesterday we had seen rabbits and deer running in the distance, and we hoped to shoot some with our arrows. Our own provisions had been spoiled by the rats that somehow infiltrated our ship. Several men became fevered from eating it. Those of us who avoided it were very hungry.

By mid-day, we had thoroughly sated ourselves. Unfortunately, the first two of our men died from their fevers by that time.

Lars, our shaman elder and strict leader, had also become ill. He could see it was going to be impossible to get our ship sailing again. It had sunk deeper into the mud, and the river, with all the silt building up in the area, had changed its course further to the south. To keep Malcolm and his men from discovering us and seeing that we failed in our mission—and losing face—Lars proposed abandoning our ship and burying it. It would take several days, and we would be susceptible to attack if Malcolm's men ventured this far downriver. Hopefully, the continuing heavy rains would keep them away. But it was a chance we had to take so we could start hiking back to the coast to one of our countrymen's strongholds. There we could board another ship home across the North Sea.

As evening came, we had already dug enough dirt and mud to encase the ship up to its prow. Also, two more men died from fever. Lars, after using his magic stick, said he felt better and ventured up the hill into the forest, presumably to keep watch for any of Malcolm's men. He did not come back.

Our numbers were diminishing, and I began to think I'd never see home again. The six of us who were well moved our dead up to solid ground and dug small chambers, lining the graves with branches and twigs, and then placing all their possessions in them, along with some food for the afterlife. The mounds increased in number as the days passed.

Lars had told me before he left that if he died, he wanted to be buried in his ship, but when we went looking for him, we could not find him anywhere in the forest. So, instead of burying Lars, we buried, with respect, our old chief, Arne Nygard, in the hold of our ship, along with all his and Lars's valuable possessions. We figured Lars did pass on out there somewhere and was taken by animals. Maybe his soul would come back to join Arne in the hereafter.

As we laid Arne to rest, I noticed that even in the dark hold, the amber of our dead sister's silver ring I now wore began to emit a glow. That seemed to only happen when Lars was near with his magic stick. My body felt strange. Tingling. Maybe it was Lars's soul telling me goodbye. I forced the ring off and placed it with his possessions.

I thought about how much I was going to miss Arne's harp playing as I placed his lyre next to his body. He always loved playing his instrument, and we all loved singing along with it. As I stood up and got ready to leave, I felt the boat shift under my feet, almost knocking me down. I rushed out of the hold to see thick wet mud oozing over the side and starting to leak into the hold. She was sinking into the soft mud even more.

As the sun went down, so did our ship. We cut the mast

and laid it on the deck, so it wouldn't stick up exposing our ship, and our location. For the rest of the evening and all the following day, we shoveled fresh dirt over it until there was a mound, like a small hill.

While we sat around our fires that evening cooking up more rabbit, we hardly spoke. We only talked about the long walk to the coast we had to begin before morning light.

Again, I still didn't sleep well, even after several day's labors. I kept hearing strange sounds all through the night. I hoped it was just the wind, but my mind feared it came from Lars's soul or maybe from the gods of the afterlife, or maybe from the underworld.

After rising and eating a little meat, we started our trek to the coast in the morning twilight. I looked back at the mounds where our fallen men lay and at the large mound where Arne slept in our ship. I sadly said goodbye to him, our shipmates, and to my missing brother, Lars.

As we left, I turned and took one last look. I thought I saw movement in the thick fog that just came in. Then I could see nothing. It must have been a deer. Maybe Lars had come back as his favorite animal. I raised my hand and said "Goodbye, Lars. We'll meet again one day."

British Museum, 1991

Thomas Stone had spent a cramped twelve hours in a flight from San Francisco to England, arriving in Heathrow late afternoon. After a fitful night in an uncomfortable and noisy hotel close to the airport, he rose and had breakfast, then took a taxi into London and to the British Museum. He wanted to see the Sutton Hoo artifacts. His grandfather,

Henry Stone, had been one of the diggers hired by the archeologist who discovered the buried ship and the many burial mounds by the River Deben estuary in 1939. The priceless artifacts Henry and others found there were taken to the British Museum after the war for study and display. But Thomas knew from his grandfather that not all of them made it to the museum.

Thomas was tall, at 6 foot 3 inches, thin, and looked emaciated even though he ate well. At forty years old, his hair was already almost all grey. He only wore jeans, blue denim shirts and hiking boots all the time. That day in London, it was cool, so he wore a shearling-lined leather flight jacket he had picked up in a second-hand store. If he had to dress up, he would add a red tie to his shirt, and slip into a brown blazer he'd picked up at the same store. Thomas was not just thrifty, he had not much money. His forklift job at one of the San Francisco docks paid little.

Thomas knew his grandfather was almost one hundred years old when notified that he had passed away. Thomas remembered while his grandfather visited him and his brother, Garrett, in San Francisco, and while "in the cups", had admitted to them that he kept some of the Sutton Hoo findings at his home in England.

Thomas didn't know about Henry Stone's death and was surprised to receive a letter from a solicitor telling him so and indicating that he inherited not only Henry's home in East Anglia, but also the contents of Henry's safe deposit box at the Bank of England branch in Ipswich. He was also surprised the letter included an airline ticket for a flight leaving the next morning and had a check with enough funds for food and lodging. He had wondered why he inherited everything and not his great uncle Garrett.

After half a day viewing the Sutton Hoo exhibit and enjoying the museum, Thomas walked a block to a local pub to have some lunch and to try some English cream ale. An hour later he took a taxi to Liverpool Street Station and boarded a train heading north. He was tired and tried to sleep on the train, but without success. When he got off in Ipswich, it was late, so he took a taxi to a small hotel that had an attached pub. He checked in, went to the pub to have a light dinner along with another pint of ale, then went to his room where he finally got some sleep.

In the morning, after the satisfaction of a full English breakfast, Thomas went to the bank. The bank building looked old, as if it had been there for over a hundred years, which it probably had. Thomas had been sent the safe deposit box key and he presented it to the man in charge of the safe, who introduced himself as Mister Johnstone. He was a short elderly man, probably as old as the bank, who wore an old fashioned black suit with a black vest over a high-collar white shirt with a bow tie. His vest had a thin gold chain that went from one small pocket to the other.

Thomas was led down a dark, wood paneled hallway and came face to face with a highly polished steel safe door, around eight feet tall and four feet wide. Mister Johnstone pulled one end of the chain out of his pocket, which had a key on it and slipped it in a keyhole on a lever. He turned the key, then the lever, and the door opened. That was it. That huge door had no combinations or timing mechanisms. Thomas followed him in.

Beyond the door was a large room with four private cubicles in the center. The wooden walls were dark oak, and each cubicle had a paneled oak door for privacy. Mister Johnstone asked Thomas to sit in the first one. He asked for his key and went into the next room to get Thomas's grandfather's safe deposit box. In a little over a minute, he returned, handed the key and the box to Thomas, and told him to press the buzzer on the desk when he was finished.

In the safe deposit box were several letters, a deed to Henry's house in Dunwich, and a few jewelry pieces Henry took from the Sutton Hoo dig. The most notable piece was a beautiful silver ring decorated with what Thomas could see as a tiny dragon holding a piece of amber in its mouth. Thomas could barely make out a very tiny insect caught in the amber. He put the ring on his finger. It fit perfectly. He put the rest of the safe deposit box items in his backpack, then buzzed for Mister Johnstone.

As Thomas left the bank, he felt an odd tingling sensation, like a slight electric shock, all over his body and got a little dizzy. It only lasted a few seconds, so he didn't think anything about it. He just put it off as jet lag.

Thomas planned to spend the next two weeks touring castles and museums in East Anglia and more touring of London before flying home. But first, he wanted to see his grandfather's house in Dunwich. What he wasn't prepared for was the location of the house.

After leaving the bank, Thomas went to the East Ipswich station to check the timetables. Within the next hour he boarded a train that ran from Ipswich to Saxmundham, which was as close as he could get by train to Dunwich.

After getting off the train, he went into a small pub. It was called the Poacher's Pocket. The place was empty except for a svelte, five-foot-four grey-haired woman behind the bar. He asked, "Can you tell me if there is a bus to Dunwich from here?"

Wiping her hands on her clean white apron, she

answered, "You can take a tour bus in the morning at ten. It loads up right in front here. Are you on holiday?"

"Sort of. I'm actually here to visit my late grandfather's home in Dunwich."

She laughed. "First, you need to say it right. Not Dun*witch*. It's pronounced Dun-ich. It's a very historic… and a very interesting place."

"Since I need to wait for the morning bus, is there someplace close where I could stay the night?"

"Right here. We have some rooms upstairs. I do have one available. Forty pounds for the night, payable now, and that includes breakfast."

"I'll take it."

"We serve breakfast from seven to nine, and you can get dinner here, too, after six this evening. Simple food that I cook, but good and filling."

Thomas signed in and paid for the room. Before the barmaid gave him a key, she looked down at Thomas's hand and said, "That is an interesting ring you have on. Did you have it made?"

"No. It belonged to my grandfather, who passed away."

The barmaid looked down at the register. "I see your name is Stone. Could your grandfather be Henry Stone?"

Surprised, Thomas answered, "Why… yes. Did you know him?"

"Yes, I did. He used to show up here usually once a week. We just heard of his passing. I am so sorry for your loss. I guess you are going to see his old house in Dunwich. Yes? Well, here's your room key. Room 2. It's upstairs and to the left. Bathroom is down the hall."

Thomas thanked her and took his small suitcase and backpack upstairs. After making use of the bathroom and washing up, he went to his room and took a short nap, waking when the scent of food cooking made him realize how hungry he was. He slipped his shoes back on and headed downstairs. The pub was nearly full now.

Not long after a dinner of fish and chips and a pint of ale, Thomas went back upstairs and dropped off into a deep sleep.

When he woke in the morning it was nearly 6:30. By the time he finished his bathroom duties and got dressed, breakfast was ready. The pub was starting to fill up with the people who were staying in the other rooms. Thomas picked up some scrambled eggs, a ham slice, and fried bread from the small steam table, and set down at a corner table. He was hungry again and quickly devoured the food.

After retrieving his luggage, he returned his room key to a very pretty young barmaid. Her smile made Thomas sigh. She was quite tall, almost as tall as Thomas, and well endowed. She had on a long white apron over tight jeans and a white t-shirt. *Is she not wearing a bra?* he wondered. Her long dark hair was pulled back in a ponytail that reached to her well-shaped derriere. He wanted to stay and talk to her, but the bus pulled up out in front of the pub and honked. All he could say to her was a thank you. He took one last look at her and smiled. She winked. He sighed and left.

The bus was half full, and the ride to Dunwich took a half hour. It stopped in front of the local museum. Thomas was the only one who went into the museum. The other passengers headed off to the coast to see the ruins of the Greyfriars Monastery.

The July day was sunny and warm. Thomas wanted to find out about the village's history, and to see if he would be able to get into his grandfather's house to see if any family heirlooms were still there. Hopefully, there will be pieces he could sell or take to an auction house. Maybe he'd sell the house. He could use the money.

The man behind the museum sales counter was elderly. His skin was tanned and wrinkled like old leather. His long grey hair was unkempt and matted, like he must wear a hat most of the time. He had a bald spot similar to a monk's tonsure. He wore a black suit that made him look like a stereotypical undertaker. He had a wide black tie hanging down from a high-collared shirt that looked like it could use a washing. He introduced himself to Thomas as Ian Malcolm. Then he said he was the mayor of Dunwich.

Thomas set down his backpack and introduced himself. "I'm pleased to meet you. I'm Thomas Stone. I've come here to see my grandfather's…"

Ian interrupted. "Ah. The Henry Stone place. Not long for this world, it seems. I supposed you want to see if there is anything in there worth salvaging before it is gone."

"Uh… yes. Gone?"

"It's very close to the cliff and might drop into the sea with one of the next big storms. You might want to hike over there soon."

"I would like to. Is that okay?"

"Why yes, of course. It is your family home. Oh, I just noticed your ring. That is a beautiful piece."

"Thank you, Mister Malcolm. It was my grandfather's."

Ian stared at the ring silently for several seconds, then looked up and said, "You should get to Henry's house before it gets too late. There is no electricity there now, so you should take advantage of the sunny afternoon."

"I will. Thank you. Goodbye, Mister Malcolm."

Thomas went to shake Ian's hand, but he turned around and headed quickly behind a sales counter. Thomas picked up his suitcase and backpack and began the quarter-mile hike to his grandfather's house. The closer he got to the house, the worse the weather seemed to be getting. He looked back to the village, and it looked calm, clear, and warm. Looking toward the house, clouds blocked the sun, and it appeared to be raining. Thomas started running to get in the house out of the rain, even though he didn't seem to be getting wet.

The Henry Stone house was small and made of large stones and with a slate roof. It looked very old and could have been one of the few original buildings left from the 1300s that survived because it had been further inland in those days. However, now it was dangerously close to the cliff, around twenty-five feet from the back of the house. Like Ian said, another large storm or two, and the house could be gone.

There was no lock on the door. Thomas went in and looked around. There was only one room. It was still furnished. At one end was a tiny kitchen with a small dining table against the wall. It had only one tall ladder-back chair with a woven rush seat. The rush was worn, and a small hole was in the middle of the seat. A low, narrow single bed was at the other end of the room against the rock wall. Its thin mattress on a wooden frame and slats looked terribly uncomfortable. Thomas set his suitcase and backpack down on the bed.

In the middle of the room was a sofa which sat across from a plain glass-front cabinet full of books, a wooden burial urn, and what Thomas figured were a few more of his grandfather's artifacts from Sutton Hoo. Next to the bed was another door. Thomas opened it to find a water closet, a tiny addition on the back of the house. It had an old-fashioned toilet with a wooden seat and an overhead tank attached to one wall, a small fiberglass shower on another wall, and in one corner, a small electric hot water heater. Thomas felt it and it was cold. The remaining toilet paper roll had unrolled making a small pile on the floor.

Thomas walked back over to the cabinet and opened it. The first thing that caught his eyes were several books on Sutton Hoo. Next to the books was a red glass goblet that had a small, forked branch sticking out of it. The goblet's stem looked like gold, and the base was decorated with green stones that looked like jade. It was in perfect condition, with no chips or cracks. As Thomas touched it, the end of the branch began to glow. He noticed his own ring was glowing too. He felt his body tingling like he was getting a small electric shock. He was scared. The earth moved under his feet. Having lived in San Francisco most of his life, the first thing he thought of was an earthquake. Then he feared that the house was falling into the sea.

He collapsed.

When Thomas awoke, he was in his bed in San Francisco. He yawned and thought he had a really weird dream. He was very thirsty, and his hand itched. As he reached over to scratch it, he saw that something was missing. His grandfather's ring was gone. His finger that wore the ring was also gone.

He screamed!

Chapter 1

San Francisco 1991

Bell and I drove to the Sea Cliff district of San Francisco to visit my Granny, Yana Blue, in her new home. Not long after returning from our adventures with our new wizard friends in the gold rush town of Volcano, she purchased the house from her old friend Garrett Stone. She moved in a few weeks ago. It was late morning and we wanted to make sure she was settled in and doing okay. However, she wasn't home.

Granny's new place was a little smaller than most of the mansion-like homes in the area. It was on a corner lot, not far from the scenic road, El Camino Del Mar. Built in the late 1920s, it was stucco, painted an olive green with grey exterior woodwork and had a newer tile roof. Her upstairs master bedroom had a view of the top of one of the Golden Gate Bridge towers. Granny wanted the second upstairs bedroom in the back as her library and writing room. We bought her a desk and some bookcases at Cost Plus, and Bell and I installed them. They covered a whole wall. I made sure they were anchored to the wall in case of another earthquake like the bad one we had a year and a half ago in October of '89. Downstairs was a great room. Garrett had it remodeled several years ago as a combined living room, with a new gas fireplace, a dining room, and a gourmet-style kitchen with maple butcher block counters. Very cozy and comfortable.

The lot was just a little bigger than the house. The backyard, barely ten feet deep, was where Garrett had planted a vegetable and herb garden. Granny wanted to continue that type of gardening, especially to grow herbs for the teas and other brews she concocted. The front yard, only about six feet between the sidewalk and the house, was a sand and rock garden with a few succulents scattered about. It was pretty, and weeds never seemed to grow there.

After we returned back from Granny's home, we were relaxing, drinking coffee, and talking about the results of the work we had done on my Haight district Victorian and the work to be done on Bell's Telegraph Hill family home. The Victorian was finally finished a month ago, and my tenants were able to move back in. We did too.

The phone rang.

I put down my mug of coffee and answered, talked for several minutes, then hung up.

"Bell, love, that was our contractor on the phone. He can't start on your house for at least a month. Maybe longer."

"Really? What's wrong?"

"He says there's too much toxic material in your old house. Asbestos and lead paint. He said there's only one company in the City who does that kind of toxic cleanup."

"Only one? Have they started cleanup?"

"Not yet. Our contractor said that company is backed up working on the old homes in the Marina. So many collapsed and were fire damaged in the '89 earthquake. A crew might be able to start next week if our contractor can get the permits in time."

"I hope so. Oh… Charles, I've got a feeling Granny is back."

"Oh yeah. I feel it too. Let's finish our coffee and head over to her place again."

Shortly after Granny purchased the house from Garrett and moved in, he stopped by to finish clearing out his gardening tools. He was about to fly off to England to live on the coast in East Anglia, in a place where he had spent the first ten years of his life. He arranged the purchase of a home in Southwold but planned to stop in Dunwich to visit his brother.

Garrett once told Granny about Dunwich. He not only told her, but he elaborated. After all, we all found out recently that Garrett had a photographic memory. He laughingly told us he was called Britannica Brain in grade school. The wizard, Dean Prentiss, who we found out was a classmate of Garrett's, verified that. Granny always said Garrett was a font of knowledge. This is what he told her.

"Dunwich. Yeah, Yana, I remember reading about it. It is often known as the Atlantis of England. I recall that it started out as a Roman settlement, then later became a Saxon settlement. By around 1100, the town and port had grown to be bigger and more important than London. There was a natural port there at the time that made Dunwich a very rich and busy city. Many churches and monasteries were built as were many stores, ale houses," he chuckled. "heh… with attached brothels, and there were hundreds of homes.

"Well, things changed quickly. The land facing the ocean eroded very easily due to soft soil. In the 13th and 14th centuries, huge storms ate away at the cliffs, causing most of the city to fall into the sea. What was once the busiest city and port on the east coast of England, became a town inhabited by ghosts. No, Yana, not real ghosts.

"Anyway, my brother, Henry, lives in one of the last of the old homes. In the current main part of the village of Dunwich are newer buildings that were built much later and further inland. Yeah, Dunwich went from a population of tens of thousands to less than a hundred in a very short geologic time."

Yes, Garrett could get carried away.

Bell and I had helped Granny move many mementos from her fortune telling business at Playland at the Beach, as well as her notebooks and other items. We had put them in the single car garage in her new home. We had a moving company take the heavy stuff, like the fancier display cabinets that came from the Mystic Eye, the shop that Granny had run with Bell's mother, Constance. Before the Mystic Eye building was demolished, we had the same moving company remove all the remaining cabinets and move them to a storage locker I rented for Granny in South San Francisco. Granny planned to sell them to another friend of hers who was going to open an occult bookshop and store in Sausalito.

Now with Granny's things out of our house in the Haight,

and after moving all my power and carving tools to store in my garage in Santa Cruz, there's now room in the Victorian's garage for two cars, end to end. My tenants don't have to find parking in the street anymore.

My name is Charles Blue. When I was seventeen, my parents were killed by a young warlock named Pete Ramahi and his mother as punishment for Granny's involvement with Pete's father's death. Granny confessed to Bell and me that Pete's father and mother were practitioners of black arts. His death, she said, came about because of the Ramahi family's plan to dominate, or exterminate, the witch and warlock communities with their own styles of power. It was war. Pete's father tried to put a death spell on Granny to get her out of the way, not knowing how powerful she really was... and still is. His own spell backfired. As far as we know, the Ramahi family is no more. Their few followers, without leaders, dispersed. The Ramahi threat was over. We hoped.

Nearly twenty-five years ago, Bell, only eighteen at the time, had been duped by Pete, who shape shifted as Granny, and put Bell into a twenty-year death-sleep. Bell finally woke and wandered aimlessly in the tunnels under Telegraph Hill. Granny sensed her, found her, and brought Bell to my home in Santa Cruz. She hadn't aged, until she began falling asleep all the time. Each time she woke up she was older, until she caught up to me. Through it all, we fell in love... again.

Now we live, quite happily, in my Victorian's third floor loft. My tenants live in the first and second floor apartments. Last week I rented my Santa Cruz Pleasure Point home, cheaply, to a University of California Santa Cruz professor and her husband. After the 1989 earthquake, it was still hard for me to go to downtown Santa Cruz because of all the destruction. And, unfortunately, my favorite hangout, the Tea Cup Chinese restaurant and bar, was damaged beyond repair and the flatiron building it was housed in had been torn down. The last I heard, Li, the proprietor and Chinese witch, and good friend, moved away to her family home in the San Fernando Valley. We've kept in contact, and she hopes to come back and open another restaurant in Santa Cruz again someday.

My Victorian house is on Page Street, a block from the Haight business district. We recently had the whole house remodeled, with all new electrical and plumbing. We got my tenants, and ourselves, new appliances, light fixtures, heating, and, for us, new furniture to replace the pieces that Pete Ramahi slashed and broke. Even though I don't play anymore, I even had my broken '57 Fender Precision Bass repaired with a new neck. Our place was very comfortable now. I had the old carpeting pulled up and had new hardwood floors put in over the old redwood flooring throughout the house. The redwood was nice and pretty, but too soft for heavy use by families with young children, like those of my tenants. I also had the exterior redone with new gingerbread trim in the front replicating what the house used to look like when it was first built, sometime before the 1906 earthquake. And finally, with a coat of new paint, the house now looked fantastic.

We were happy with the contractor we hired and wanted him to continue working with us on Bell's Telegraph Hill home once all the hazardous waste could be disposed of. Fortunately, the cost of the hazardous waste removal will barely dip into Bell's inheritance, an inheritance left to her by her mother, Constance. After Bell's mother passed away, Granny had a friend reinvest Constance's large cache of stocks, bonds, and money, and it had done very well.

The underground shaft and tunnel connected to Bell's house would also get filled and compacted. The original tunnels, and the rooms where Chinese slaves lived and the graves of a few of them, had been explored and catalogued by University of California archeologists and students. There were a few other connecting tunnels, blocked by cave-ins, that the archeologists discovered and are still exploring. Bell and I were anxious to hear about what they find in there.

It was noon when Bell and I arrived at Granny's place again. She greeted us with hugs.

"It's always nice to see you two lovers come by. I just got home."

"We know, Granny. Bell and I felt your return. We came here earlier and could not contact you or feel your presence anywhere."

"Ah. That was because I was south in the Santa Cruz Yacht Harbor having tea with my friend Gwyn. Her boat is shielded from telepathic interference. But with her psychic ability, she knew you children were at my house looking for me. I came back after we finished talking and drinking our tea."

We talked with Granny another fifteen minutes then said we had to go. As we got ready to leave, her phone rang. Granny asked us to wait a minute while she answered it. She talked for several minutes, writing down some information, then came to see us off.

"That was Garrett," she said. "He's calling from the inn

he's staying at. It's called The Ship. It's in that village on the east coast of England called Dunwich. He says he got there to find that his brother was gone, and no one knows where he went. The innkeeper told Garrett that he hasn't been there for a week, and he usually came in every afternoon for a drink. Odd, too, Garrett said he also found out that his nephew, Thomas had a reservation there two days previous. He had no idea Thomas was in England. But he never checked in. A couple of the locals told him they remembered seeing a tall, thin stranger with a suitcase and backpack walking down the street toward the Stone house. They suggested he might have gotten too close to the cliffs and fell and maybe washed out to sea. Garrett went down to the beach and used his warlock abilities to look around but saw nothing out of the ordinary except for very thick fog. He then went back to his brother's house again to see if he had shown up. He said the door was open and he thought his brother had returned. He was still not there. Then he felt that someone broke in. A cabinet was open, but he couldn't see if anything was taken."

Bell commented, "I hope Garrett's brother and his nephew are okay and maybe just traveling together." Then after thinking about it, she asked, "Yana, does Garrett's nephew have any powers?"

"No. He doesn't. Garrett had told me that Thomas's father, Robert, was adopted by Henry Stone during the war. Robert was mortal, and not long after he married, Thomas was born. Oh, I just remembered, Garrett asked for me to check out his nephew's apartment for something Garrett had left with him for safe keeping. It's one of his last journals. It might have some sensitive information in it. He told me the apartment's manager has a key and called him to let him know we were coming. Charles, can you drive me there? It's in Cow Hollow, just up from the Marina district."

After Granny changed into some warmer traveling clothes, we all climbed into our van, fastened our seat belts, and headed across town to Cow Hollow.

When we arrived at the apartment complex, there was nothing on the building indicating who the manager was or what apartment he lived in. As we were reading the names on the doorbell panel, an elderly gentleman came out and smiled at Granny. I could see in his twinkling eyes that he thought Granny was an attractive woman, and he wanted to know her. I think Granny blushed. She could see it too. Bell and I smiled at each other then asked, to be polite, who the manager was. Thanks to our telepathic abilities, we already knew it was him. We introduced ourselves, and he introduced himself as Tony Macintosh.

"Call me Mac. Anyway, Thomas's uncle… what was his name? Oh, yes. Garrett. He called me and said Thomas was missing. I was worried about him, so I went up to his apartment to check and heard noise inside. I knocked. He didn't open the door, but he told me he was home. I just figured he had been sleeping or just got out of the shower. He sounded odd. His voice was high, like he might be tired. Maybe jet lagged. Then I saw him leave just a half hour ago. I said hello, but he seemed preoccupied and didn't reply. He had a hooded sweatshirt on with the hood up. He seemed in a hurry and disappeared in a thick fog that had just come in. He's always been a model tenant. I knew he went on a trip to England, and said he'd be gone two weeks, but he must have come back early. He was gone only a couple of days. I was surprised he was home."

I was thinking, and Bell and Granny heard my mind, "*So was this a wasted trip?*"

Granny answered, telepathically, "*No, we did find out that Thomas is back. It is strange he made a reservation in the same inn Garrett is now staying in. That's really odd. I'll call Garrett and let him know his nephew is back.*"

Mac was gazing at us and wondering why we were just looking at each other and not saying anything. We all caught on right away and apologized.

I said, "Sorry Mac. I think we were all wondering why we were asked to come here if Thomas was already home. It's just a little confusing. We were supposed to pick up Garrett's jour… a book of Garrett's that Thomas has in his apartment. Hopefully, he'll be back soon."

"Yes. Like I said, I was surprised he was back. Do you want him to call you when he gets back?"

"No. He should really call his uncle in England… well, maybe early morning. It's probably two or three in the morning over there right now. Granny, here, has the number. You have a pen or pencil for her to write it down?"

"I'll get a pen and paper from my apartment. I'll be right back."

For someone who looked as old as Granny, he was pretty spry and trotted up the steps.

Bell nudged Granny in jest. "Yana, he likes you. His eyes look kind, but a little sad. I see he's a widower. Maybe four years now."

"Now Bell, I'm too old to have another man in my life."

Bell grinned and put her hand on Granny's shoulder. "Now Yana, you're never too old."

We were all chuckling as Mac trotted back down the stairs and gave Granny a pen and note card. She wrote down the number and handed it back to him.

"Thank you so much, Yana. It was wonderful meeting you." Mac reached over and shook Granny's hand. It looked like he didn't want to let go, but finally did. Then he turned to us, a little flustered, and said "…oh, and you two. Goodbye, and have a safe drive home."

When we dropped Granny off at her house it was late afternoon, and my stomach was growling.

"I'm starving. What say I head over to Clement and pick up some burgers from Bill's Place and bring them back. Uh… Granny, they have vegetarian burgers too. Want one? With fries?"

"No," Granny replied. You two go there on your own. I have plenty to eat here. Charles, you two got me more than enough food from the store to last me weeks."

"You sure Granny? You don't want us to bring you something back?"

She answered me telepathically. *"Go. Enjoy your time together. I'm fine and comfortable here."*

"Okay Granny. If you need anything, anything at all, give me a call, and we'll pick it up for you."

"Go!" Granny was smiling as she shooed us out.

Bill's Place is one of the few remaining old family burger restaurants in the area. When I first tried their bacon cheeseburger, I vowed to never go to a chain burger joint again. It was love at first bite. When Bell first tasted one, she said it spoiled her for any other burgers.

By the time we got there, the main business lunch crowd was already heading out. We ordered our burgers, with fries and colas and got a table by the window. We were both so hungry, we almost inhaled our food. We were done before we knew it.

We drove back home fully sated and with hamburger onion breath and parked in front of my house. Since everything that happened in 1989, and what I've learned since then, I set a spell to always leave a parking space directly in front of my house. It has been a game changer. No more searching for parking in the neighborhood.

As we got out of the van, Elaine, who was one of my tenants, came out of the house cradling a baby in her arms.

"Charles, UPS dropped off a couple of packages for you. They're both a little heavy. I have them just inside the door."

"Thanks, Elaine, I think Bell and I can take them upstairs."

"You sure? Tom is home today and could help if you want."

"Nah, we got this."

Bell and I went up the porch steps, pulled the boxes out of the apartment entry, mouthed a quick incantation, and the boxes were as light as a feather to us. I thanked Elaine and the two of us walked around to the back of the house. We accessed our loft apartment by the fire escape stairway in the back.

Once inside we set the boxes down. I saw the return address. *Ah, Computerwise.* They often send me samples for me to try out and review in my A. Techman column in the Computerwise tabloid. Since moving all my computer gear up from Santa Cruz, I now write my column here, which is better since the Computerwise office is in downtown San Francisco at the Flood Building. I don't have to fax hardcopies anymore. I just put it on a floppy disk and drop it off at the office.

We opened the boxes. The first had a new PC and portable in it, a Commodore, and an Apple Powerbook. The other had a complete Compaq system with a thirteen-inch color monitor. The Commodore only came with a keyboard and a mouse. I'd have to use my own color monitor to test and review it.

When we remodeled the loft apartment, the large side closet, previously used to store boxes of Granny's old photos and knickknacks, I had converted into an office. The carpenters raised the ceiling and put in a window and skylight. I moved my desk from Santa Cruz and put it in my new sunny office.

Up until a few months ago, I was still working at Stor-tech in Milpitas. Unfortunately, I was let go, as was everyone else. The company couldn't compete with the newer innovative disc drive companies and went belly up. I knew that was going to happen, but I wasn't sure when. It finally did. And as much as I hated to do it, I sold my commuter car, my Miata, last week. Bell and I didn't really need two cars to maintain and pay insurance on.

So now I'm able to spend more time on my computer column, and more time with Bell, who plans to travel with me to computer shows in LA, and, of course, here at Moscone Center. She also sometimes helps me with the column. I like to hear her take on the new technologies.

The phone rang.

"Hello?" I answered. "Patrick. Good to hear from you. How are you doing? How's retirement?" Patrick English was an ex-homicide detective who had helped us deal with the Pete Ramahi situation. We also bonded over Patrick's newly discovered warlock abilities.

"I'm doing okay. And retirement got boring. Yesterday I applied for my PI license."

"Really? That's great, Patrick. When do you get it?"

"It'll take a few weeks or more. The state does

background checks, which should be no problem for me having been a homicide detective for thirty-plus years. The hard part will be the hand-written test. Tests make me nervous. I've always had trouble with tests my whole life."

"Hey. That shouldn't be a problem at all. Especially since you have better abilities now. You can use that to relax yourself."

"Ah. You just reminded me. I'm supposed to meet up with Yana for another lesson in an hour. However, the reason I called is that I was talking to Lieutenant Castillo… you remember Castillo, don't you?"

"How can I forget. Last time I saw him he actually smiled and greeted me like an old friend."

"Yeah. He's been a happy camper ever since you did your shaman thing on him. Well, anyway, I was talking to Castillo, and he told me he was investigating a body that surfaced in the water in the East Harbor by Fort Mason. It seems to have floated up from under a large sailboat docked there. It's a guy who was supposed to be in England. He did fly out of SFO just two days ago, according to the airline records, and he still had his return ticket in his pocket when found here. Castillo asked if I could help. I'm asking you if you'd like to help. This all sounds a little, how to say, mystical."

"Really? Uh… Patrick, do you know what his name is?"

"His wallet was still in his pocket. His driver's license says Garrett Stone."

Chapter 2

Garrett! It couldn't be! Granny's oldest friend! She just talked to him!

My mind was racing. I shook my head in disbelief then noticed Patrick was still speaking to me on the phone. "…when I went to see Yana for a lesson last week, Garrett was with her. She introduced me to him. I liked him. She said they've known each other for over seventy years. He was there to pack up the last of his things to put in storage before he left for England."

"Pat… Patrick." The lump in my throat made it hard to talk. I took a deep breath, put my hand on my medicine bag to center myself, then was able to continue. "This does sound, like you said, mystical. Uh…Something's not right here. Granny just spoke to Garrett in England a few hours ago. He told Granny that his nephew, Thomas was missing, but he showed up at his apartment when he was supposed to be in England. Why don't you come on over here for dinner around six and we can talk… more about it." I was choking up again. Try again. "Patrick, Bell and I came across something similar today. Garrett's nephew, Thomas, showed up at his apartment when he was supposed to be in England."

"That does sound odd… and similar… except he's alive. Right? I want to hear all about it. I'll let you know when I'm coming over so you can lower your protection spell." We both said our goodbyes.

I told Bell about Garrett, and we both held on to each other for several minutes with tears in our eyes. I dreaded telling Granny but knew I had to. Bell and I went to her house. She took it hard. We all cried together.

It was nearly 5:30 when Patrick called to say he was heading over to our place. Bell had gone out after we got back from Granny's and picked up some groceries at the Haight Street Market. The two of us were preparing a one-pan lemon chicken mixed with fettuccini, zucchini, red peppers, and onion. It was a dish that my parents used to make when I was young, and Bell said her mother used the same recipe but with an Alfredo sauce. It made my mouth water just thinking about dinner. I pulled a bottle of a good cabernet out of the cupboard.

Bell got the telepathic message from Patrick that he was parking a block away and should arrive shortly. Bell and I held hands and mouthed the protection release so Patrick could come up with no problem.

As soon as he was in, Bell and I held hands again and reinstalled the protection spell. Patrick watched us as if he was trying to learn all he could about incantations and spells. "Yana has been teaching me protection spells. It seems the easiest so far for me to learn. Yeah, I know. After two years I'm still trying to get used to this way of life."

"You're doing fine, Patrick," said Bell. "By the way, are you hungry?"

"Famished. I had a late breakfast and no lunch. And something really smells good."

I poured wine for the three of us, and we sat around just talking about current politics, Patrick's application for a PI license, and how his warlock training has been going. We didn't want to talk about Garrett until after dinner.

The lemon chicken was slow cooked and shredded earlier, and the veggies were done. Bell put the fettuccini in the boiling water. Once it was al dente, she drained it and put it in the pan with the other items, mixing it together with a jar of Alfredo sauce, then served it up in large bowls.

While eating, we didn't even talk. The food tasted so good. Bell and I laughed to ourselves as Patrick kept oo-ing and ah-ing as he lifted each forkful into his mouth.

Finally, after dinner, and a second glass of wine for each of us, we got serious and to the subject at hand.

"Patrick, Bell and I were asked by Garrett to go over to his nephew, Thomas's, apartment to get Garrett's journal. What took us by surprise was that the landlord said Thomas was back already, after only a couple of days in England. We did a little digging, and the airline, British Air, has a record of him flying to England, but no airline has a record of him flying back. The same thing happened, as you mentioned, to… Garrett." I felt myself choking up again. Medicine bag time. I sighed and continued. "However, Garrett ended up in the water. We have no idea why."

"So, you're saying these two, Garrett and Thomas, might be connected somehow?"

"It appears so. Same family. They both went to England, to the same village, to visit the same house. We should ask Castillo for us to see Garrett's body with you."

"Maybe we can use some kind of incantation to get him

to accept you two as consultants."

I smiled at him. "No, Patrick, that won't be necessary. I have my medicine bag on me. Remember, that's what I used to cure Castillo from his panic after seeing us take care of Ramahi. All we need to do is show up, and Castillo will be glad for our help. Also, we need to find Thomas. His landlord said he left his apartment before we got there."

"Why don't we all head over there tomorrow morning around ten." Patrick suggested. "Give me the address and I can meet you there."

Bell cut in. "Hey guys. Yana's calling."

Patrick questioned that. "You mean telepathically?"

The phone rang. I picked it up as Patrick chuckled in the background. "Hi Granny. You doing okay? Yeah. Sorry. I know. We were just talking about that with Patrick. You want to go too? Okay, Bell and I will pick you up around 9:30. We'll meet Patrick there at ten. Love ya, Granny. So sorry… about Garrett. See you soon. Bye." Choking up again.

"Granny took it really hard about Garrett, but she's also worried about Thomas. He has no powers at all, and maybe he had an encounter with magic, and it might have messed up his head. We need to find him so I can use my Ohlone medicine bag to soothe his mind."

Patrick looked thoughtful. "Hmm. You know, it is getting late. I better get home and get some sleep so I can think clearly tomorrow. Sleep off that fine food and wine you served me. I have a feeling this problem might escalate. Yeah. It is a strange feeling for me. I'll see you all tomorrow at ten."

With that, Patrick left.

Bell asked me, "Do you get that feeling too? That this

might escalate?"

"No. I really don't have a feeling like that. What I'm feeling now is that someone is blocking my thoughts. And I know it's not Granny. I can't…"

Before I could finish talking to Bell, I got an immediate rip-roaring headache, blacked out, and collapsed on the floor.

Somehow Bell got me to bed, which is where I woke up over fourteen hours later. I glanced at the alarm clock and saw it was nearly two the next day. When I glanced the other way, the first thing I saw and felt was a very worried Bell holding my hand. The headache was gone, but I felt like I'd been the recipient of a heavy-duty spell. I felt weak and could barely raise my arms.

"Bell. Hand me my medicine bag, please."

"I've been so worried. I called Yana right away. She was here and tried to help, but nothing worked. We thought you were not coming back. I've been holding your medicine bag against you for eight hours. Here."

I took the bag and put the cord back around my neck. Holding the bag with my right hand, I put my left hand on my head, and mouthed an Ohlone healing spell. Again, I pictured my grandfather, Peter Red Feather, and immediately felt revived. I threw the covers off and jumped out of bed.

Now I was worried about Bell. She looked like she hadn't slept.

"My love. Don't worry about me," she said. "We need to figure out what happened."

"All I remember when I passed out, I felt someone, or something, shoot through my body. It felt like my head split open. Hell. We had protection spells on this house. What got in?"

"I felt nothing in the room when you collapsed. I usually feel a presence if there's one there. Nothing! Even the whole time you were out, I felt nothing around."

The phone rang again. Bell answered it.

"Hello? Oh… Castillo? Uh… nice to hear from you. You sound upset." Bell could always sense the caller's feelings. "What? Really? Patrick is missing?"

"Yeah. He called me yesterday saying he was supposed to meet both of you at the yacht harbor, but said you cancelled it. He planned to go anyway to look over the crime scene, then meet with me at the station. He never came in," Castillo said from the other end of the phone. "I called his home number several times and got nothing but a dial tone. So, I drove to his place and the door was closed but unlocked. His apartment had been turned over. Everything was scattered like someone was looking for something. I brought forensics in, and we couldn't get any fingerprints. None, other than Patrick's."

Bell was silent a few seconds and looked over at me. I knew something was wrong. She continued talking to Castillo. "He was just here last night having dinner with us. He left about ten and said he had to rest up for a meeting with us at Garrett's nephew's place this morning. Uh… Charles woke up not feeling well and we couldn't meet Patrick." True. Sort of. I just never woke up. "Garrett's nephew is missing too."

"Balls on a duck!" An uncharacteristic exclamation from Castillo. "Uh… sorry, Bell. I know Patrick considers you and Charles as good friends… and good investigators." I was holding my medicine bag with my eyes closed. I could see Castillo. A little incantation, and he needs our help. "I could use some outside help. Your help. Why don't I meet you at that guy's nephew's apartment. Say in two hours?"

Bell gave him the address, said goodbye, and came over and gave me a big hug. "You feeling okay now?" she asked. "Yes? Then take a quick shower, 'cause you really stink," she smiled at me. "...then put some clothes on your handsome body." She looked me up and down and winked at me.

Less than two hours later we arrived back in the Cow Hollow district. Once again, it was hard to find a parking place, and we ended up parking three blocks away in a parking garage on Lombard. We hurried over to Filbert and saw Castillo just getting out of his car. Somehow, he found a parking place nearly in front of the apartment. I was jealous. I smiled at him as I told him so.

"How did you get this parking place? We had to park way the heck over on Lombard! Any word on Patrick? No? Crud. Let's find Mac."

No sooner did I mention his name, and Mac appeared and greeted us. Castillo introduced himself and showed his badge then asked him, "Has this Stone guy showed up yet?"

"Sorry to say, he hasn't shown up since he left yesterday. I know you want to check out his apartment. I've got the master key here. I'll take you upstairs and let you in. Follow me, please."

We followed Mac upstairs and he unlocked the door to Thomas's apartment. When he opened the door, we were met by a scene of disarray, like Patrick's place, according to Castillo. The apartment was completely torn apart. Chairs and a sofa were tipped over. The large Oriental carpet was rolled up and pushed against the wall. The small portable television was face down on the floor, and we could see that the kitchenette's drawers were pulled out and their contents scattered all over the place. Several knives look like they were thrown around and a couple were stuck in one of the cabinets.

We were all in shock. Castillo finally spoke. "Uh… Mac, didn't you hear any of this going on? This kind of mess must have made a lot of noise."

I don't think Mac heard Castillo. His mouth was open as he walked around scanning the damage.

"MAC!" Castillo yelled and got his attention. "You didn't hear this happening?"

"N… no. I didn't. I'm here all the time. I should have heard this. What happened? Where's Thomas?"

Bell and I were looking around and noticed something odd about the rolled-up carpet. I touched it and felt another headache coming on. I winced. Bell asked, "Are you okay?"

I didn't answer her. Holding on to my medicine bag to ease the pain, I called Castillo over and pointed to the carpet.

"Lieutenant Castillo, I think Thomas is in there."

We carefully unrolled the carpet, and, sure enough, there was Thomas. His body was dried up and wrinkled like he had been dead a while. Bell and I were thinking about looking for the journal, but Castillo had said not to touch anything. He headed out to his car to radio for forensics. Unfortunately, Mac was getting sick seeing the body. He left too, leaving us alone to gaze at the body and wonder how and why this happened.

Bell and I took a better look at Thomas. We noticed he had a missing finger. A rough scar showed where the finger had been. There was also dried blood on his head.

Castillo came back in. "When I called forensics and mentioned this guy's appearance, they told me when they brought that Garrett fellow to the morgue, he looked the same. Kinda mummified they said. They'll be here shortly. I also called in at the precinct. Still no word on Patrick."

"Damn!" I exclaimed. Then I asked Castillo, "Hey. Who did Mac see leave this apartment? It couldn't have been Thomas if he's been wrapped up in that rug." Then I said telepathically to Bell, *"Hope it's not another assassin or shape shifter like Ramahi."*

"I really hope not." I could see the worry on her face.

Castillo looked thoughtful and was stroking his mustache. "Maybe it was the murderer who the manager saw."

"Mac said when the guy who he thought was Thomas left, he wore a hooded sweatshirt. I'm sure Mac didn't see the guy's face. Also, Thomas looks pretty tall. You should ask Mac if whoever he saw was as tall as him."

"Yeah. I'll do that. Say, I'll also ask Mac if he has any security cameras around this building."

"Good idea. My Granny used to have one in her old store. Hopefully, Mac has... ow!"

Another headache was coming on, so I quickly wrapped my left hand around my medicine bag, turned away from Castillo, closed my eyes, and mouthed an Ohlone healing spell. That helped. I spoke to Bell telepathically.

"Bell, There is some kind of weird magic happening here. And it's somehow affecting me but not anyone else in the vicinity. And where is Patrick? I'm worried about him. Yes, I know you are too. I don't know what kind of magic this is or where it's coming from. We've got to talk to Granny."

"Yes, we should. As soon as Castillo's forensics team arrives, let's head out."

When the team arrived, we told Castillo goodbye and good luck. We reassured him we would be available to help if or when he needed it.

Just before arriving at Granny's house, I tried to give her a telepathic message. What I heard from her sounded like a telephone answering machine. Bell heard it too.

"I'm not home right now. If you want to talk to me, please leave a message."

"Uh… Granny, where are you going?"

No answer.

"She must have taken a taxi," I said to Bell. Taxis, with their two-way radios always on and connected to dispatchers, made it hard to converse telepathically. The radio waves somehow blocked the ability or created a lot of static in your head.

We arrived at Granny's house and parked across the street.

"Let me see if I can determine where she is." Bell unfastened her seat belt, leaned forward, and put both hands flat against her eyes. She was moving her lips, but no sound came out. I could see she was mouthing an incantation. Then she opened her mouth and only the sound of static came out. "Ouch! Damn! That hurt."

"What happened?"

"Yana *is* in a (cough) taxi. I started to get a fix on it, but it must have gone into a (cough) tunnel. The taxi's radio (cough) produced a bunch of static. It hurt my ears and (cough) my throat." Bell coughed again then cleared her throat. "Anyway, the taxi's position seems close. Maybe it was going through the Park Presidio tunnel."

"Say, she might be going to Fort Mason to see where Garrett ended up. Maybe she's going to try scrying. She could have something of Garrett's she can use."

Bell looked at me askance. "Scrying? I never learned anything about that. Did you?"

"No. Granny told me about it when she was trying to teach me spells when I was in college. You remember, I was not the best student in the world back then. But I do remember her saying that to scry, you need something owned by whoever you want to find something on or about."

"Why don't we go to the Fort Mason harbor and see if she's there."

Bell refastened her seat belt, and I drove off, heading east on Lake Street to Park Presidio, where we impatiently sat for what seemed like ten minutes before the light finally changed and I turned north, entering the tunnel that runs under a section of the Presidio. Exiting the tunnel, the first thing you see is the Golden Gate Bridge looming ahead. But we were not heading to the bridge. We turned right toward the Marina, merged into the bridge traffic, and quickly moved to the far-left lane. Within less than a mile, we exited onto Marina Boulevard. Our next turn was across the street from the Marina Safeway market. We drove through the harbor parking lot and found an open space right away. A taxi was parked at the corner of the lot. It looked like the driver was napping.

"That must be Granny's cab." I pointed. "Let's go ask the driver if she was his passenger."

We got out and walked over to the cab. The turbaned cabbie, a light-skinned Sikh with a full black beard, had his head back and his eyes were closed behind his dark glasses.

I tapped on his window. He awoke with a start and rolled down his window. "What you want?" He sounded angry. "My cab is not available."

"Sorry to bother you. Did you bring a little old lady here?"

"What's it to you? Leave me alone!" He started to roll his window up. I mouthed a simple incantation and his window stuck halfway up.

"The lady is my grandmother. I'll ask again. Did you bring her here?"

"Okay. Yes. I'm to wait for her. Now leave me alone."

"Thank you, sir," Bell said with a little edge on her voice.

I mouthed a few words and the cab's window closed the rest of the way on its own. The cabbie's blue turban almost flew off as he jerked his head back in fright.

Bell and I walked over to the edge of the harbor looking around for Granny.

Bell suggested, "Let's try to contact her telepathically now that she's out of the cab."

"*Granny. We are here at the harbor but can't see you anywhere. Let us know where you are.*"

Still no answer.

"Charles, maybe if she's scrying, she doesn't want to be disturbed."

"I hadn't thought of that."

I felt a tap on my shoulder. It scared me and made me jump forward and turn around, ready to protect us from whoever it was.

It was Granny, who somehow snuck up behind us, and sheepishly said, "Oops. Sorry, Charles, dear. Didn't mean to scare you."

I took a deep breath then gave her a hug. Bell did the same, and said, "Yana, we were worried when we couldn't contact you. I tried to locate you, but the cab's radio interference caused static in my head."

"I knew you'd finally figure where I was, but I had to keep my mind quiet for my little scry job."

"What did you use?" I asked.

"Garrett didn't put everything in storage when he moved. He left one of his old briar pipes on the gardening bench. I found it the other day and was going to send it to him. I'm... I'm sorry to say he won't be using it anymore." A tear ran down her cheek. She sighed. "Excuse me, dears, I need to go pay the cabbie for his time, and you can drive me home."

Forty-five minutes later, we were sitting around Granny's living room sipping tea and eating packaged cookies. She started explaining what happened.

"Patrick gave me the idea to look for the place Garrett showed up. I had the cabbie drive along the parking area by the harbor until I told him to stop. I got the feeling magic happened really close. The metal door to the dock was locked, but easy to unlock, like you can do so well, Bell. I went down the dock to the spot Garrett was found. There was a two-masted sailboat docked there. He... was found wedged between the boat and the dock. The name on the boat is *The Anglo Saxon,* and it's from Dunwich, England."

Bell asked, "Dunwich? That's significant, maybe?"

"Yes, it is. Yes, it's the place both Thomas and Garrett were visiting. Now let me continue before you ask any more questions. I used Garrett's pipe. I was able to scry... well, very little anyway, to try to see what happened. I only saw him flying to England. Nothing about his showing up here."

"Do you think it might have been another type of assassin?" I asked. "Someone who can do some kind of spatial transference. Bell, remember those time trips in

Volcano? We became extremely thirsty after each one."

Granny continued, "Maybe that's what happened to Thomas after he showed up in his apartment. And maybe someone killed him then wrapped him in his carpet. Whoever it was might have been looking for Garrett's notebook. We need to talk to… uh, Mac once more. Also get into Thomas's apartment again. Questions?"

Bell spoke first. "If Garrett's notebook was there, could Castillo's forensics team have taken everything?"

"I'm hoping Garrett did like I did with my notebooks and put protection spells on it. Let's hope it got missed."

"Granny, none of your notebooks, or Constance's, had anything about scrying. Did you ever write anything about that?"

"No. Scrying is hard to describe or teach. I tried with you once, dear, but…"

"Yeah, I know. Too young. Too impatient."

"Yes, you were, dear. Anyway, Bell, it's a way of seeing a single person's past events, usually only one per article of clothing or item, like the pipe. The only way to really instruct how to scry is to see it in action. However, very few of us can scry. Let's go back to Thomas's apartment and see if we can find an article of his to take with us."

"To England?" Bell and I both asked.

"England. I will scry in Dunwich. But first, we need to locate Patrick."

We were silent a few minutes. All of us were deep in thought. We then decided to visit Patrick's apartment right after we checked out Thomas's once more.

Chapter 3

After we finished our tea and ate nearly a whole package of chocolate chip cookies, we headed back to Cow Hollow. Again, parking was abysmal. I dropped Granny off in front of the apartment building, then Bell and I drove around the neighborhood until we found a parking place large enough for our van, two blocks away.

By the time we walked up the steps to the apartment house, Granny was already inside the front door being entertained by Mac. They were both laughing.

Mac saw us at the door and let us in. "I'm afraid I've been boring Yana with my life story. I guess you're all ready to go into..." Mac started to choke up. "...uh, Thomas's apartment. I'll... I'll just give you the key if that's okay. Oh, by the way. Detective Castillo... uh... he asked if I had a security camera. I wish I did... but, uh... but no."

Granny put her hand on Mac's shoulder and mouthed some soothing words. He sighed and smiled at her. I could see he was upset about seeing Thomas's body and having such a horrible thing happen in his apartment house. He was also wishing Granny would keep touching him.

Mac gave me the key and we walked up the stairs to

Thomas's apartment. It was still in disarray. Only the carpet was missing. Castillo's team must have taken it along with the body. There was dark fingerprint dust on every surface. Only a few fingerprints were showing. Bell glanced at them. "These are days old. Thomas's. I don't sense any others."

We started looking around for some article of clothing or other item not touched by Castillo's team. Granny told Bell and me that if someone else has handled anything of Thomas's, scrying wouldn't work. Unfortunately, all clothing from the closet and dresser drawers had been scattered on the floor.

"Granny, I'm beginning to think there's nothing here you can use."

"Maybe, but we haven't looked in the bathroom yet."

The medicine cabinet was open, and everything taken out and scattered in the sink. Several containers of pills, vitamins, and other medicines were opened and dumped. Why? We had no idea.

Bell noticed something. "Yana. Charles. The toothbrush is still in the hanger. It looks like it hasn't been touched." Bell started to reach for it. Granny stopped her.

"Don't touch, dear. Only I can touch it. If you or Charles touch it first, it won't work. Oh. Look here. A comb. Still has hair in it. I'll take both of them just in case."

Granny picked them up with a piece of what looked like yellow cheesecloth then wrapped them in it.

"Granny. What is that you're wrapping them in? Cheesecloth?"

"It is, but I've soaked it in a neutralizing agent I brewed. That keeps the items in their last used state. That will last long enough for us to get to England to scry with them. Now. Let's see if we can find Garrett's notebook."

We were disappointed. Granny shook her head. "It's not here. It's either well hidden, or whoever trashed this place might have taken it. Let's go find Patrick."

I was the last one out and locked the door. Mac was still standing downstairs at the entrance and lit up when he saw Granny walking toward him. Bell and I looked at each other and smiled. Mac was definitely smitten.

"Y…Yana," he stuttered. "I…I hope I can see you again sometime."

Granny took Mac's hand and smiled at him. "We're going to England soon, but we can visit when I get back."

I sensed Mac's heart beat a little quicker. "Goodbye, Yana. Please have a safe trip… and a safe return."

Even Granny seemed reluctant to let Mac's hand go this time.

"Granny, Bell and I will go get the van and come back to pick you up."

And ten minutes later we did just that and headed over to Patrick's apartment.

Patrick lived on the corner of Chestnut and Laguna in the Marina District only three blocks from Thomas's place. The apartment building was built in the 1930s but remodeled in the 1950s in the modern style of the time. If it was just me and Bell, we would have kept the parking space and walked. But with Granny along, we drove the short distance. However, just like nearly everywhere else in the City, parking was again a chore. Once more, I dropped Granny off in front of the apartment building while Bell and I looked for a parking place. Luckily, a place opened up a block away on Laguna, close to Lombard.

When we walked to the entrance of Patrick's building,

Granny was talking to a woman who looked almost like her doppelganger—same diminutive size, shape, hair length and color. However, she was dressed much nicer than Granny. Her below-the-knee-length black dress fit her well. A wide red belt was around her waist, and she had a hand-knitted red shawl around her shoulders. Her low-heeled shoes were also red and highly polished. No scuffs.

"Bell. Charles. This is Madam Hopkins. I've known her since my fortune telling days. She was also a fortune teller, but in the Fishermen's Wharf area. She used to come into the Mystic Eye to visit me."

Bell and I said we were glad to meet her.

"Please call me Ann. Like Yana, my fortune telling days are long gone, but I keep my hand in a spell or two once in a while." Her smile and twinkle in her eyes were just like Granny's.

"Ann lives here in the building," Granny explained. "She said she'd help us find Patrick. She lives across the hall from him and knows about his limited abilities, but he doesn't know about hers. Yet."

"I'll take you upstairs," Ann said. "If you need me to unlock Patrick's apartment, let me know."

"Thank you, Ann, but we can manage. Bell is very good at that."

"Our little elevator only holds two people. Yana and I will go up then you can press the button to bring it back down."

"No problem," I said. "Bell and I can take the stairs."

When the elevator door closed, Bell and I started up the stairs. We got to the third floor just as the elevator arrived. Slow lift. Granny and Ann got out, and she led us to Patrick's apartment.

Bell was about to unlock the door when both Granny and

Ann said to stop. They looked at me with concern. I closed my eyes tightly. I was getting another rip-roaring headache.

Bell noticed it too and quickly lifted my hand to my medicine bag. I saw Grandfather, Peter Red Feather. I thought I imagined him placing his hand on my head. I opened my eyes and felt fine. I told Bell to go ahead and unlock the door.

Granny spoke to all of us telepathically. *"Hold it a minute, Bell. Ann and I sense a presence that's moving around in there. No, it's not Patrick. Whatever it is, it must have affected Charles but not us."*

Ann also spoke telepathically. *"This is new. There's never been a presence like this in this building. Wait!"* Ann then spoke out loud. "It's gone!"

"Go ahead, Bell, you can unlock it now," Granny said.

Bell spoke a couple of words in silence, turned the doorknob and opened the door.

What greeted us was another apartment in disarray. Castillo told us Patrick's place was a mess, and it was. A sofa and easy chair were turned over. The television cabinet was on the floor and the screen was cracked. A bookcase was tipped over and its contents were scattered. At least the carpet was still in place. The attached kitchenette's drawers were pulled all the way out and tipped over. Again, like Thomas's place, knives were tossed around. One was stuck in a cabinet door that was half off its hinges.

"Holy sh... I mean holy cow!" I exclaimed. "What the... what's going on? Granny, Ann, you both sensed something, and whatever it was had given me a serious headache. Hey. I wonder if this 'thing' has something to do with Patrick missing."

We heard the elevator door open down the hall.

I realized the apartment door was still open. Before I could run over and close it, Ann said something in French and the door closed on its own and locked.

We started to look around for more damage when we heard the door unlock.

It opened.

We all yelled at once.

"PATRICK!"

"What the hell happened here?" Patrick looked at us as if we had something to do with the mess. His voice rose with anger, and his hands tightened into fists. We were shocked to see him, and he was just as shocked to see us. Looking at him, it appeared like he hadn't bathed or shaved for a while. His white shirt was dirty, and his blazer was too. It also had a torn side pocket. His khaki slacks looked like he'd been rolling in mud, and his right knee was torn. He also had a black eye, like he'd been in a fight. He was getting more agitated.

I held onto my medicine bag again and said a few words in Ohlone. I then walked up to him and put my hand on his shoulder. Patrick asked again but more calmly, "Blue, what happened here?"

"Patrick, you don't know how glad we are to see you." I swept my hand around the room at everyone there. "Before we tell you about this, what happened to you? You've been missing for over a day."

"Are you serious? I just left here to meet with Castillo a few hours ago."

Granny came up and put a hand on his other shoulder. "Dear Patrick. Have you looked at yourself lately? I think you should go look in the mirror."

"Wha…"

"Go, Patrick." That was from Ann.

He shrugged and walked into the bathroom.

"WHAT! THE! HELL!"

He came back out, tipped his easy chair right side up, and sat down with a thump. I could see tears forming in his eyes. Time for my medicine bag again. He calmed down once more.

"I look like I've been in a fight. I don't remember it though. What happened? What's been going on? Why… uh… Ann, why are you here too?"

"I'm sorry, Patrick. Yana and I are old friends. You might say we are birds of a feather."

Patrick looked confused, then leaned back and calmly said, "Hmm. You know, you do look alike. You're not sisters, are you?"

"Only sisters in spirit," Ann said. "I keep my background secret from the other tenants here, but you're different now. You've become one of us."

Granny cut in. "Now. Patrick, give me something on your person. You have a pen? Pencil? Notebook? Anything in your pockets at all?"

"Uh… why? Are you going to do something I need to learn?"

"Maybe. It's called scrying. I take something that belongs to a person and can visualize what happened. No, you probably couldn't learn this. Very few have the ability to scry. Ann, can you do it too?"

"No. I tried a couple of times, and nothing happened. I've never known anyone but you who could scry."

"Patrick?" Granny pulled out another yellow piece of cheesecloth.

"Okay," Patrick said as he rummaged through his pockets. "I've got my wallet. That's it."

"Do you have a hanky?" Granny asked.

"Uh… yeah, but it's used."

"Perfect. Pull it out and drop it in this cloth." He did. "Charles, please set the sofa upright so you all can sit down. But please be very quiet and turn off your telepathy. I can't have any disturbances."

I turned the sofa over and pushed it back to the wall across from Patrick. Granny sat down on the floor directly in front of him. She put a hand on his knee, said some words in Romani, and Patrick's eyes closed. Bell, Ann, and I sat quietly watching.

Granny opened the yellow cheesecloth exposing Patrick's well used hanky. She said some words in Romani and closed her eyes. She pressed the hanky to her forehead and went into a trance. We watched as her body swayed back and forth, side to side. It was hard not to think or say something, so once more I grabbed my medicine bag to keep myself quiet. I closed my eyes.

With my eyes closed, I suddenly saw what Granny was seeing. Patrick had been at the yacht harbor to check out the place where Garrett appeared. He was captured. How, I can't see. He was put to sleep… no, hypnotized inside the sailboat. He had an out-of-body experience. He… no, his mind was transported. England? Coastline? He woke back on the dock here in San Francisco. He tried to get up, got dizzy and fell, tearing his clothes and hitting his eye.

Granny opened her eyes.

"Uh, Charles, dear, what did you just do? I felt you join me."

"I have no idea what happened. I just held on to my

medicine bag and closed my eyes, and there you were. I was seeing what you were seeing."

"Oh, my gods and goddesses! Maybe you can scry! Somehow Peter Red Feather's medicine bag helped you."

"Don't you remember, Granny, I used it to enter Patrick's mind before when Pete Ramahi was using telepathy on him that sounded like you? I think I got in Patrick's mind again while you were there this time."

Patrick woke up. "What happened? Yana? Why do I feel so tired… and thirsty."

"Patrick, dear, do you remember going to the harbor a day ago?"

"A day ago? I thought I went there a few hours ago. Why is my body sore?"

Granny said, "Bell, could you get Patrick some water? Charles, after he has some water, I think it's Grandfather time again."

I understood right away. After Patrick chugged a pint glass of water, I walked over to him, touched his shoulder with one hand while holding my medicine bag in the other, and spoke several words in Ohlone. Patrick leaned back and closed his eyes.

"He'll sleep for an hour or two, then be fully refreshed and healed when he wakes."

"Charles, dear, I'll stay with Patrick and make sure he eats something. You and Bell should go home for now. Ann, thank you for letting us in. Let's get together again soon for tea and talk."

"You are so welcome, Yana. Please contact me if you need any help with these strange happenings."

With that, Ann walked out, crossed the hall, and entered her own apartment.

"Granny, you going to be okay? I see you're a little tired from scrying. You want me to use my medicine bag on you too?"

"No, dear, I'm okay. My energy will be back by the time Patrick wakes up. I want to make sure he gets cleaned up and eats, then he and I will talk more. Hopefully, he'll remember more of what happened to him after he wakes. Now, you two lovers, get on home and rest. Tomorrow we must go to that boat again and look around. Whatever we find there, I'm sure it will point us to England."

Chapter 4

It was almost six the next morning when I awoke with another bad headache. I reached for my medicine bag, said a couple of Ohlone words, and it went away. Then I heard Granny's voice in my head. Bell did too. She woke up. Granny was contacting us telepathically.

"Dear ones, Patrick and I talked most of the night after he woke and got cleaned up. I got a few hours of sleep on his sofa. He's up already, feeling great, and cleaning up the mess. Patrick will drive me home, then he's going to go see Castillo. He's making coffee and oatmeal for us right now. Pick me up at my place at nine."

Bell and I looked at each other. She said, "Well, I guess we should get up and have some coffee and oatmeal too."

At nine I parked our van in front of Granny's house. Before I could get out of the car, she came out in a hurry carrying her carpetbag. I barely had time to open the sliding door for her to get in the back seat.

"Granny, do we need to pick anyone else up? Patrick?" I started the van and headed back down Lake to Park

Presidio.

"No. Patrick will meet us there after he talks to Castillo. He wants to let Castillo know that he's alright and was suddenly called away on a family emergency. That's the story we agreed on this morning."

Commute traffic was still heavy coming south off the Golden Gate Bridge heading into the City. It was hard maneuvering the van off the Park Presidio ramp onto 101 and across all lanes so we could get off on Marina Boulevard. I made some commuters in their shiny Volvos and Mercedes throw up one-fingered salutes as I sped up to cut in front of them. The Marina turnoff comes quickly.

I again turned into the Fort Mason Harbor parking lot across from the Marina Safeway.

Five minutes later we were at the gate of dock G14 just as a fog drifted in. It was so thick we could barely see past the gate, which was locked. However, it was easy to open with Bell's help. We walked through the fog down the dock to the slip where the boat sat... or had sat. The slip was now empty. The boat was gone. The fog cleared and the bright sun was almost blinding.

"Well, well!" Granny exclaimed. "It seems we're too late."

We stared at the empty slip in silence for a minute.

Bell broke the silence. "Yana, the harbor office is right over there." She pointed across the harbor to a small building on a wide dock off the Fort Mason parking lot. "We could ask them who rented this slip."

"Good idea, dear."

This was a long walk to the harbor office, and Granny was starting to get winded. She put her hand on my shoulder to support herself. I grabbed my medicine bag and felt Grandfather again. It was like he also helped support

Granny, and she stopped breathing hard and was keeping up better.

We finally reached the harbor office only to find it locked. A plastic clock dial inside the door's glass said back at 11. We would have to wait at least fifteen minutes. Fortunately, there was a bench in front of the office. We started to sit down to wait, but a tall, thin attractive woman, probably in her forties, was walking toward us on the dock with a grocery bag in her hands. She was fashionably dressed in a dark blue double-breasted blazer with a red patch over her left breast that had two anchors embroidered on it with one word stitched over them: Aweigh. *Hmm. Anchors aweigh? Sure.* I had to laugh to myself. The blazer was over a white high-collar blouse with a frilly front. She wore tight-fitting black slacks. The one thing that was not fashionable were scuffed up white fabric deck shoes.

"Sorry to keep you waiting," she said. "I was at Safeway getting something for lunch." She unlocked the door. "Please come in." She sat her grocery bag and purse down on her desk. "My name's Bridget. Bridget O'Leary. What can I help you with?"

Granny introduced us then answered her. "We were supposed to look at a two-masted sailboat on dock G14, but it's not there. Can you tell me who rented the slip it was in, and where it came from?"

"Well, I'm really sorry, but I can't divulge that unless the renter let me know you were interested in the boat."

Granny mouthed a few words in Romani.

Suddenly, Bridget was ready to divulge everything. "Two-masted sailboat. There are no two-masted sailboats at that dock. What slip?"

"Number 11," I told her. "Who rents that one?"

She reached behind her and pulled a large account book from a cabinet. She thumbed through it then pointed at a blank line.

"No one has rented that slip for a month or more. We save a couple along that dock for guests who arrive by boat to rent on a daily basis."

"Oh. Well, we're so sorry to have wasted your time, Bridget. I guess we were told wrong about the sailboat."

"No problem. You might check to see if the sailboat is in one of the other harbors. Oh, if you'd like, I share my office with a yacht salesman. He could find you a two-master if you're looking to buy."

"Thank you, but no, Bridget," Granny said. "We have an appointment we have to get to." Sort of true. We were supposed to meet Patrick at the dock, and he hadn't shown up yet.

We walked back to dock G14 and did find Patrick standing outside the locked gate looking in. When he saw us, he shook his head.

"It's gone."

"I know," Granny said. "We were just at the harbor office, and they have no record of any boat in that slip for months, and there's never been any two-masted sailboats docked here, according to the lady at the office. I think we're dealing with magic, Patrick, that you got caught up in. Thank the gods and goddesses you didn't end up like... G...Garrett." Granny looked down and sighed.

Patrick shook his head again. "I thought our episodes in the tunnels was as weird as this warlock stuff could get. Now this!"

"We'll find out what's going on, Patrick," Granny said. "I promise you."

Bell suggested, "Let's all go back to Yana's so we can plan our strategy."

The four of us sat around Granny's living room sipping tea, regular store-bought black tea, not Granny's herbal concoctions.

Granny started the discussion. "The town of Dunwich must be the link to all these events. Garrett went there. His nephew, Thomas went there. The sailboat's name showed it's from there. If that boat is real."

"The boat has to be real," I said. "We've all seen it. Including the police when… uh, Garrett's body was found. If it isn't real, it must be a very advanced spell for everyone to see it."

Granny looked deep in thought.

"Uh… Granny, what?" I asked.

"This is new. What happened to you on that boat, Patrick, is something I've never known to happen before. It is not a type of spell anyone from our small community of witches and warlocks could do. Or would do."

Bell cut in. "Is there anyone in our… uh, community who might be able to help? Who might know about this type of magic?"

"Only our wizard friend Dean Prentiss over in Volcano, but he's too busy with his family, dear. We might be able to find…" She sighed. "Well, maybe my sister in England could help."

I nearly dropped my teacup. "Sister? You have a sister? I have an aunt in England?"

"Great aunt, Charles, dear. She's your great aunt."

"Holy cow, Granny, how come you've never told me about her?"

Bell and Patrick were curious and were leaning forward to hear it all.

"It was her idea to keep it quiet, especially after she got married to a mortal and moved to England. She had two children there, girls, who are both grown, married, and are competent young witches. After her husband passed away, she opened her bookshop, Atlantis. When we go to London, you'll recognize her right away. We're twins."

"Twins?" Bell, Patrick, and I said at the same time.

"So, are we going to England right away?" I asked.

"Yes. I'm sure our answers are there. We can do nothing more here in San Francisco. Patrick, do you want to go too?"

"I'd better stay here for now. I might get my PI license this week, and I promised to help Castillo on the Thomas and Garrett Stone mysteries. He told me yesterday he's hit a brick wall. Forensics hasn't been able to come to any conclusions about the break-in or the body at Thomas's place. Of course, they would never understand what happened. Anyway, I'll take a look. Maybe I can 'see' more than forensics." Patrick used air quotes.

"Possibly," Granny said. "I'm sure you can't scry, but you may be able to sense something there. Don't force it. Relax and just let it happen. Believe in it. And, whatever we find out in England, we'll keep you in the loop. Do the same for us."

"Telepathy?" Patrick asked.

"Telephone," Granny answered. "Too far away for telepathy. When we get settled in London, I'll call you. I'll do the same when we get to Dunwich. Bell, Charles, you should go home and get ready for our trip. Pack for at least ten days. I'll call my travel agent and order our plane tickets. Patrick, stay for a few minutes more. I want to teach you one more thing."

Bell and I said our goodbyes, jumped in our van and drove home.

Two days later, we picked Granny up at 8am and drove to the San Francisco airport. I let her off in front of the international terminal with our suitcases then drove to long-term parking. By the time we got back to the terminal, Granny already had one of the curbside porters check our suitcases in.

Bell and I each had backpacks with an extra change of clothes along with some bottled water, and cheese and crackers to snack on. Granny also had her satchel, the bottomless carpetbag with many changes of clothes. It was also carrying her scrying items from Thomas's apartment, plus a thermos of herbal tea.

Finally, it was time to board the plane. When they announced for first class to board, Bell and I just sat there, thinking we would be called later, but Granny stood up and motioned for us to come along. She purchased first class tickets for us all. She wanted to be comfortable on the long trip.

As soon as we settled into our roomy first class seats, Granny put on the complementary sleep mask and slept most of the way, only waking for meals. Bell and I tried to nap too, but we were too excited to sleep. Besides, the stewardess kept coming by plying us with champagne. Five hours into the flight, and we both felt a little tipsy.

Not only were the drinks nice, the meals on the flight were great. In first class the British Air food was as good as what you'd get in a fine restaurant. They even had vegetarian meals available, which Granny appreciated.

Almost thirteen hours later, we landed at Heathrow. We retrieved our luggage and caught a cab into central London.

Granny had contacted her sister before we left San Francisco and she made reservations for us at a hotel, just a couple of blocks from her bookstore. Granny told the cabbie to take us to the Russell Hotel in the Bloomsbury district.

It took a good forty-five minutes to get to the hotel. Bell and I both got nervous with all the cars driving on the "wrong side of the road" so to speak. When we pulled up to the front of the hotel, two doormen in Beefeater-style outfits ran up to open the door for us. They loaded our suitcases on to a baggage trolly and pushed it inside.

The hotel was gorgeous. It was a 19th century edifice with four statues of queens on the second-floor front wall looking over all who entered below. After we passed under the royal four, we checked in at the front desk, and a bellboy, or rather bell-old-man, took over pushing the trolley and took us in the elevator to the seventh floor. He opened the door.

It was a gorgeous two-bedroom suite. The bellboy showed us around, pointing out the lavatories in each bedroom, which were big enough for a king size bed, a love seat, and a dresser. The living room was a little larger and had a camel-back sofa and two easy chairs with light blue velvet upholstery. Burgundy colored pillows accented the furniture. A writing desk by one of the windows overlooked the park across the street.

On the walls were several 19th century oil paintings of horses. Horses racing. Horses jumping. Horses in a fox hunt. Too many horses if you ask me.

Fresh vases of flowers were on the surfaces in every room. Even the two bathrooms.

Granny tipped the bellboy, who's eyes went wide when

he saw how much she gave him.

"Big tipper, Granny? I think you shocked that poor bellboy." Bell laughed.

"Let's get unpacked. Afterwards, we can go downstairs to the restaurant and get something for dinner. Then we should get some rest. Tomorrow will be busy, my dear ones."

Chapter 5

Because Bell and I could barely sleep on the plane, we were extremely tired and went to bed an hour after dinner. We had slept for nine hours when Granny finally woke us up. It was seven in the morning.

"Get up, dear ones. It's about time for breakfast to arrive."

Granny seemed bright and perky. Well, she did sleep a lot during the flight.

Feeling jet lagged, Bell and I struggled to get up. Or rather Bell struggled to get up to use the bathroom before me. After she came out, I rolled out of bed and went in to do my duties and turn on the shower. This bathroom had a large shower with two shower heads next to a fancy clawfoot bathtub.

"Bell, want to join me in the shower?"

"Thought you'd never ask."

After spending way too much time in the shower, we finally let go of each other, dried off, got dressed and went into the living room. Granny had ordered breakfast from room service—oatmeal for herself, and full English breakfasts for me and Bell. I didn't realize how hungry we were. I ate the bacon, poached egg, fried mushrooms, a large sausage I think was called a banger and the fried toast. Bell ate all but the mushrooms and only half of the banger. I ate the rest of it.

It was nearly ten-thirty when we finally left the hotel for Granny's twin sister Sybil's Atlantis bookstore. Granny called her earlier to let her know we would be coming.

It was a short two-block walk. Bell and I were both surprised when we went in. It was not a regular bookstore like we thought, but an occult bookstore and magic shop, kind of like Granny's old Mystic Eye. Granny only told us her sister had a bookstore. She didn't say what kind.

We walked in and the first thing I noticed was how big Sybil's shop was. It was easily twice the size of the old Mystic Eye. The ceilings were ten or twelve feet high and covered with decorative tin tiles. It also had the wonderful smell of old books and herbs.

Bell and I could see how much Sybil looked just like Granny. Same face. Same thin shape. Same long white hair tied up in a bun. Same smile. Same twinkle in her eyes. The only difference was in her clothes. Where Granny wore her usual loose-fitting beatnik-style grey sweatshirt and jeans when traveling, Sybil wore a black turtleneck tucked into black, tight pants tucked into almost knee-high black boots with two-inch heels. That put her taller than Granny's five foot one.

Sybil came out from behind the counter and gave Granny a huge hug, then worked her way to Bell then me. She gave tight hugs. I grunted.

"It's so wonderful to see you again Yana. Charles. Even our London community has heard so much about you and Bell and your wonderful abilities."

I blushed. Bell said, "Thank you. It's so nice to meet you."

Inside the bookstore were several easy chairs where people could relax while reading, sipping tea, or talking. Bell and I sat down together in a very comfortable leather loveseat, and we all gabbed for several minutes. Sybil asked Bell and me about our adventures, and Granny and her sister tried catching up on family matters.

Finally, Granny said, "Sybil, you know why we're here. You knew Garrett, didn't you?"

"Oh yes. I knew Garrett. You remember I met him when I visited you in San Francisco some… oh. So long ago. Fifty years, is it? Well, recently he came in here to visit before traveling to Dunwich. I heard… uh…" I could see Sybil was a little choked up about Garrett. She cleared her throat and continued. "Sorry. I heard through our witchy grapevine what happened to him. His nephew too. I am so sorry. I know Garrett was a real good old friend of yours."

Granny looked down and sighed. I think I saw tears forming again. After clearing her throat just like her sister did, she continued, "What can you tell us about Dunwich? Have you heard of any other strange occurrences happening there in the past?"

"Yana, dear, there are more stories out of that part of East Anglia than I can tell you. I'll tell you one that really stands out. It has to do with the lost city. One of the buildings that fell into the sea back in the 14th century belonged to a couple, a warlock and witch. The rumor is that instead of vacating the building when it was about to be destroyed, they stayed and fell into the sea with their house. Others say they may have escaped the house before it crashed into the sea or became haunting spirits. Some even believe they have seen their spirits."

I had to ask. "Have any of our kind ever seen them? Could these people not be spirits and still be living in Dunwich?"

"That I do not know. No one in our community knows."

"What about Garrett and Thomas?" Bell asked. "Have there been such disappearances in Dunwich before?"

"This is the first time I've heard about it happening to a warlock like Garrett, but mortals, like Garrett's nephew, have been known to disappear from the area before, so I've heard. I hope it's not true. I know the three of you are going to Dunwich tomorrow. Be extra careful. Here." Sybil handed Granny a highly polished green stone. "Take this to add to your own stone for added protection."

"What stone are you talking about?" I asked, looking from Sybil to Granny inquisitively.

"Our family jewels," Granny chuckled. "Really, each member of our family has a protection stone. Mine is red, actually an uncut sapphire. Sybil's, as you can see, is green jade. Our brother's was blue sapphire."

"Brother?" Bell and I both said together.

"I haven't mentioned him to you before because he passed away unexpectedly many years ago around the same time you lost your parents. It appears he might have been hit by the Ramahis too. He had a small typewriter repair shop in downtown San José that burned down… with… him in it."

"That sounds like the Ramahis alright," I said sadly.

For the next hour Bell and I listened to Granny and Sybil catching up on old times. Bell said to me telepathically, *"You know, I get the feeling we should visit the Sutton Hoo exhibit at the British Museum. Garrett had mentioned that exhibit to Yana. Let's walk over there and check it out. Maybe we can get some kind of feelings from the artifacts there."*

Before I could answer, Sybil cut in, "*Good idea, dear ones. It is an interesting exhibit. Yana and I have much more to talk about.*"

Granny then added, "*Yes. You two go and see if there is anything you can find out.*"

Bell and I said our goodbyes and left Atlantis. We knew that Granny and Sybil wanted to talk more in private. More secrets, probably.

Thirty minutes later we were at the British Museum. When we arrived at the Sutton Hoo exhibit room, only one other person was in there staring intently at some of the artifacts in a large glass display case on the wall. He was dressed like my grandfather Peter Red Feather in an old-fashioned funereal black suit with a high-collared white shirt and black tie. He held a black top hat in his very wrinkled hand. He was not tall. A few inches shorter than me and Bell. When he sensed us, he quickly turned away and walked briskly out of the room.

"That was strange," Bell said. "I sensed that guy has powers. We have to describe him to Sybil and see if she recognizes him."

"Yeah. I sensed that too. Let's check out what he was looking at so intently."

We walked up to the window to where the guy stood and looked in. Bell and I both shivered. I felt like I was getting another headache and quickly grabbed my medicine bag to soothe my head.

"You okay, Charles?"

"I'm okay now. I really want to know why this is happening. I just looked at that..."

"It's a ring just like the ones we have on. Look. The same tiny griffin holding an amber piece. And... Jeez, Charles, isn't that a shriveled finger next to it?"

A ring. A finger. No descriptions. I kept staring at them, then it came to me in a flash. Actually, the ring flashed in our eyes nearly blinding us. And both of our rings were glowing. We felt a little electric shock. Somehow, our rings made me realize that the finger was Thomas's.

Bell and I stared at the finger and ring for several minutes, not saying a word. Both of us had been holding our breaths as if breathing or saying anything would break a spell. That flash of light that made me see Thomas also showed me a rock house in Dunwich. Garrett's brother's place? Nothing else. I felt I was scrying, but I wasn't touching anything like Granny does. I just looked at it.

Finally, Bell whispered, "I felt what you felt, but I couldn't see it like you. Where did you go?"

A young family came into the room, so I had to answer Bell telepathically. She responded, *"We really need to find out why it's only you who keeps getting headaches. I get the feeling it has something to do with Dunwich... or maybe even Sutton Hoo. I think we should head to Dunwich as soon as we can. I know Yana wants to go too, but she also wants to visit with her sister. Hope we can convince her..."*

Bell paused, because just then we both sensed Granny. She was entering the museum along with Sybil. Barely a minute later, they were standing next to us.

"Sybil felt an odd disturbance. It came from here. We got worried and hurried over. What happened?"

I related seeing the funereal-suited guy then looking into the case and the finger and ring, then getting another headache, a flash, and the vision. *Did I leave anything out?*

More people were coming into the museum and drifting through the Sutton Hoo room. Sybil spoke to me telepathically. *"Charles, dear, what caused your vision?"*

"Look." I pointed at the finger and ring. *"Do you see what I see?"*

Sybil looked and gasped. Granny looked and said, *"Okay. We must leave for Dunwich tomorrow. Sybil, can you help us find a train that goes there?"*

"I doubt if one goes to Dunwich, it's too far out of the way. I'll call one of my friends who works at Kings Cross station."

"Thank you, Sybil," Granny said, giving her sister a hug. "That will be a great help. When I get back to London, we'll talk more."

We didn't have to wait long for the information. Sybil called within the hour. Her friend checked the timetables and told her what train we should take and where to make a transfer to take us as close as possible to Dunwich. We would take one train from Liverpool Station north to Ipswich, then after a two hour wait, transfer to a small single-car electric train to Saxmundham. From there we'd take a bus to Dunwich.

The next day, by nine in the morning, we purchased our tickets and boarded the train to Ipswich. Seven hours and two transfers later we made it to Saxmundham.

Not knowing where to catch the bus to Dunwich, we walked a block to The Poacher's Pocket and went into a low-ceilinged classic pub that must have been around for hundreds of years. The two-story building had whitewashed plaster walls below a heavily thatched roof. Inside was all dark oak. Oak paneled walls, oak booths, tables, and chairs. The only bright area was a well-lit shelf of spirits behind the bar. We were the only ones in there.

Behind the bar was a fair-skinned man with a bushy black beard. His long black hair was tied back in a ponytail. His bare arms were covered in colorful tattoos of dragons, unicorns, and Celtic symbols. He was just a little taller than Granny. He looked as old as her.

Granny took one look at him, he looked at her, and to Bell's and my surprise, he came out smiling from behind the bar and gave her a big hug. Granny noticed our curious expressions.

"Sorry, my dears. This is Tobias Durban. We knew each other in San Francisco. He had arrived from England and got a job working as a maintenance man at Playland when I started fortune telling there. We dated a short while." I thought I noticed Granny blush. "No, Charles, I wasn't with your grandfather yet."

Tobias, in what sounded like a Scottish accent, asked Granny, "So where is the old Indian? And this guy here is his grandson? Ach… *powers*?" That last word was spoken telepathically.

"Many, dear Tobias, he has all of mine and more. He also has the Ohlone powers of Peter Red Feather. The late Peter Red Feather. Yes, he passed on several years ago. Anyway, Charles may not look it, but he has done wonders."

Now it was my turn to blush.

"And with Charles is sweet, dear Bell. I don't know if you remember Constance Beltane. She also worked at Playland but in the office. She became my partner in the Mystic Eye."

"Aye."

"Ah, you do remember. Constance was Bell's mother. Yes, Bell here also has incredible powers." She put her arm around Bell. "Now, dear Tobias, we need to take a bus to Dunwich."

"Dear Yana, the next bus won't leave for Dunwich until noon tomorrow. Uh… I have a couple of rooms upstairs you can have… for the night… gratis for you, Yana." Tobias looked away. I noticed a frown. He turned back with, what looked like to me, a forced smile. He asked Granny, "So, what happened in Dunwich that brings you all the way here to the English sticks?"

Bell and I sat down in a wooden booth while a very animated Granny told Tobias the whole story. He listened intently, but I had the feeling he already knew about what she was telling him. By the time she finished with her narrative, several people, locals we assumed, had come in and sat down. Tobias had to excuse himself to wait on them. Granny came and sat down with Bell and me.

"Tobias said that his wife, when she gets here, will get us some food."

As she said that, a young couple, a tall, husky blond man and a tall pretty woman with long black hair, came in the door behind a woman who looked Granny's age. She went behind the counter and kissed Tobias on the cheek. Tobias came over to us and said his wife arrived to do the cooking. Her name was Eve. He then spoke to us telepathically, *"Eve… doesn't know about my powers and our background. Please don't mention anything about it or us or… anything."*

"Don't worry, Tobias. Silence is golden."

"And here are your menus. Eve's kitchen here is limited, but she makes tasty fresh roasted chicken sandwiches."

We were all very hungry, only having snacks on the train and at the station in Ipswich. I said, "That sounds great. That will do me fine."

Bell agreed. Granny didn't eat meat, so she asked for a grilled cheese sandwich.

Two hours later, after good food and two pints of ale. Tobias escorted us upstairs to the rooms. In each one there was a double bed, a dresser, and a single easy chair. That was it. The shared bathroom was down the hall. Tobias said no one else was currently staying there.

After two pints of ale, I fell asleep right away, waking up at 6:30 am to the sound of Granny knocking lightly on the door. Bell was sleeping soundly and didn't hear her. Granny spoke through the door telepathically. *"Charles, dear, Tobias told me last night that he has heard about the strange happenings in Dunwich. His very small community here says there's some kind of spirit making trouble. Tobias offered to drive us there in a couple of hours. He wants to help us look into it."*

"Okay, Granny. We'll get up and get ready," I said out loud. I went over and kissed Bell on the forehead. She stirred, opened her eyes, and smiled up at me. She stretched. When I mentioned what was happening, she quickly jumped out of bed.

We dressed and got downstairs to see Granny and Tobias were already sitting at a booth talking. Bell and I sat next to them and tried to listen in. However, Eve walked in carrying a tray of food, so everyone clammed up. Eve had made very standard American-style breakfasts for me, Bell, and Granny—two scrambled eggs, bacon, and toast. I told Eve how I appreciated not having a huge full English breakfast again like we had in London. She smiled, but her eyes looked sad.

An hour later we loaded our luggage in the back of Tobias's Land Rover Defender and took off for Dunwich.

Chapter 6

When we arrived in Dunwich, it was barely 10am, and it was foggy. In fact, most of the drive was in fog, which got thick enough to slow us down as we approached our destination. Fortunately, Tobias knew the road well enough, and we soon pulled up in front of the town's museum. Next door was The Ship Pub and Inn where we were going to stay. The same place Garrett had been.

Tobias said, "We might have to wait a short while for the mayor to arrive."

Just then, we saw the sign in the door's window turn from closed to open. I didn't see any hand turn it. *Okay. Time to go in and meet the uh… mayor.*

The four of us walked up the thirteen steps… yes, I counted them… to the landing in front of the wide oak paneled door with a half-length beveled glass window. Tobias opened the door for Granny and Bell. I followed them. Tobias walked past us, I figured to introduce us. However, no one was in the museum, but I felt a presence there.

Finally, a door opened on the side wall behind the front desk and out came the mayor. It was the guy Bell and I saw in the Sutton Hoo room at the British Museum. He was wearing that same black funereal-looking outfit. He half-smiled as Tobias reached out to shake his hand. Odd, I thought. The mayor looked like he was reluctant to shake Tobias's hand.

"Well, Tobias, it has been a long time since we…"

He cut his greeting short when he noticed the rest of us. His eyes were impossible to read, and he looked a little shocked to see us. He gathered his composure quickly.

"Ah. Tobias. Introduce me to your… friends."

He did and introduced the mayor as Ian Malcolm. Mr. Malcolm didn't shake any of our hands but bowed politely to Granny and Bell. He just nodded in my direction, without looking at me. I was feeling another headache coming on and grabbed my medicine bag to stop it. I had an odd feeling about this so-called mayor.

Somehow, he must have noticed my discomfort and thoughts. "I am not a real mayor. It is just what the locals started calling me because… I've lived here longer than most of them, and it stuck." He was talking to Granny and Bell and kept them between him and me. He seemed to be avoiding me for some reason. I noticed Ian had the same type of accent as Tobias, who stood by the door, leaning on the wall, watching the interaction intently.

"Excuse me, Mister Malcolm." I was trying to get his attention. He didn't look at me but replied.

"Yes. Please call me Ian."

"Yes. Ian. We wanted to know if you met either Thomas Stone or Garrett Stone. They both came here to Dunwich to visit their relation's home."

"Hmm." Ian paused, like he was thinking of what to say. "I usually remember visitors who come in the museum." He was talking directly to Granny and not to me. His answer was vague. No yes or no.

Granny caught on quickly. "Say, Ian. Can you possibly take us to the Henry Stone house today?"

"I cannot. I have to stay open here for the tourists. A busload should arrive soon. I can point you in the right direction though. The house is easy to find. You can walk there."

Ian showed us maps on the wall of Dunwich before it disappeared and how it looks now, with dotted lines delineating the original shoreline several hundred yards out in the ocean. Close to the current cliff was the Stone house. There was a dirt road running off the main road that led to it. Tobias said he'd drive us over so Granny wouldn't have to walk there.

"Be careful on that road, Tobias. It can be treacherous if wet."

I looked out the window. Clear. The fog was gone and there was not a cloud in the sky. While Tobias, and Ian talked, Granny was still looking at the maps, and Bell and I walked around the museum to check out the exhibits. There was a cabinet with artifacts found at the Greyfriars monastery, and another with pieces of old sunken Dunwich that had washed up on the beach. One cabinet housed jewelry, pottery, and glassware supposedly from Sutton Hoo. All replicas.

"Charles, another ring." Bell pointed at it and spoke in a whisper. It was just like the one at the Sutton Hoo exhibit in London, but I experienced no strange feelings looking at it.

"Fake. These are all replicas. Odd, though, this style of ring seems so out of place with these other jewelry pieces. The bracelets and other rings look like they were hammered into shape and with minimal decoration, like runes, carved in them. That ring, like the one in London, was cast. A lost-wax process like these of ours you made."

"You know, now that you mention it, that's why the ring in the Sutton Hoo room looked out of place too. It must have a spell on it the way it affected you there. I'm worried why it hits you and not me or Yana."

"It's worrying me too. I was beginning to think I was getting some kind of brain disorder. My medicine bag helps each time. I get the feeling Grandfather is watching over me."

"That's a good thing. Peter Red Feather was a wonderful man… and spirit."

Tobias and Ian finished talking, and Tobias said that we should go.

"Ian was very closed mouthed about any goings on at the Stone house. Charles, I noticed how he avoided you for some reason."

"Probably because we saw him in London at the Sutton Hoo exhibit. He avoided us there too."

"I've known Ian for years. Sometimes he's very friendly, and sometimes he's very private and angry. I've even seen him when he's trying to cast spells. It's like he's possessed."

"Maybe that's what he was doing in the British Museum," I said as we all climbed into the Land Rover.

During the short drive, the weather made an abrupt change. The wind came up, and it started raining. Tobias felt the road might be slick, so he put the Land Rover into four-wheel drive.

When we arrived at the old house, the rain was coming down hard but didn't seem to be hitting the car. Before we got out of the Rover, Granny tapped Tobias on the shoulder and said to him telepathically, "*This is Ian's work, isn't it?*"

"*I don't think so, but if we all work together, we can stop this.*"

Bell and I heard that and agreed. Granny and Tobias turned to Bell and me in the back seat, and we all held hands. Granny started saying words in Romani, Tobias said words in English, as did Bell. I copied Granny's words. The rain stopped and the sky cleared again. We all breathed a communal sigh.

"Okay," Tobias whispered. "I think we're safe for now. But keep a look out for anything that feels wrong."

We all got out and walked up to the front door. It was closed, but not locked. In fact, there was no lock on the door.

Before we went in, Granny did one of what I used to call her touchy-feely things. Instead of touching someone, she touched the side of the house with her eyes closed. She shivered.

I asked, "Granny, you okay?"

"Yes, Charles, dear. I was just doing a little scrying. I got a bit of a shock to my system. This house has been cursed. Could have been by Henry Stone. Maybe that is the cause of the strange happenings with Thomas and Garrett. We need to all work together again to clear our way in."

Just like in the car, we all held hands and spoke our own words. Granny touched the house again and closed her eyes. "That weakened the spell, but it's still too strong to enter safely. We have to do it once more."

We repeated our anti-spell words once more. Granny again touched the house, in a different place, and said it was now safe to go in. Tobias pushed the door open, and we entered.

We looked around to see if we could find any evidence of Thomas or Garrett having been there. Nothing. The place wasn't dusty, so no footprints could be seen. It looked like it had been cleaned recently.

We started to open cupboards and drawers. When we got to the display case against the wall, we all felt a tingling, like a slight electrical charge. My headache came back. Time, once again, to grab my medicine bag. *Thank you, Grandpa.*

It was clear that one or two of the artifacts in the cabinet had power on their own. Granny opened the cabinet. A red goblet was next to an urn. *Henry's ashes?* Granny picked up the red goblet. She asked for quiet, then began scrying with it. At one point, she had to catch her breath and her legs almost buckled under her. She started to drop the goblet but caught it before it could fall.

"Granny! You okay? Yes? What did you see?"

"I saw Thomas. I saw Garrett. I saw…"

"What did you see?" Bell, Tobias, and I asked at the same time.

"So many people! There have been too many over the years, no, decades, that have been transported from this place. Most were mere mortals who broke in trying to steal something. There were one or two warlocks too. Also, this goblet had something in it. Recently, too. Henry Stone must have had strong powers to put so much protection on this place. You'd think Garrett would have been immune or could counter his own brother's spells."

Tobias put his arm around Granny. "Like you said, this maybe is my… uh, Ian's work. I've known him, and I've known his moods. He blows hot and cold, warlock wise."

"No. This is not his doing. I'm not sure if it's even Henry's."

"Granny, could you see anything else?"

"A little. These few artifacts are ancient. Henry was a

digger at the Sutton Hoo archeological site and snuck some of his findings off the site. He sold most to private collectors and kept his last few in the cabinet."

"You got all that from scrying?" Bell asked.

Granny half smiled. "No. Garrett told me about his brother's history many years ago. I didn't see that in my vision."

Feeling more at ease, we started looking around for anything that might have been left by Thomas and Garrett. The single main room showed no evidence. I opened the door to the water closet, and it was another story. Besides smelling of backed up sewage, probably from a full septic tank or broken pipe, there was an empty backpack that had been pushed or thrown to the back corner next to the toilet. I didn't want to touch it. I called Granny.

She came in, took one look, pulled another piece of coated cheesecloth out of her satchel, grabbed the backpack, and took it into the room. She began scrying again.

"Yes. This is Thomas's. And guess what? This was in a bank... hmm. Odd. Thomas was willed this house and contents. You'd think Garrett would have inherited it. Well, this backpack held the title to this house and a few antiques... a couple of Sutton Hoo artifacts. We should see if Ian knows anything about this."

Tobias looked concerned. "I've always known Ian is peculiar, but I've tried to keep a decent relationship with him. If you need to confront him, I need to stay out of it. I don't want to upset him. He knows where I live, and he knows... my wife. She has to be ignorant of all this."

"Don't worry, Tobias," Granny assured him. "We'll take care of this."

"I'm sorry, dear Yana, I can't help. Is there anything else

you want to see here before we check you into The Ship Inn?"

"I want to look outside around the house," I said. "This place is hundreds of years old. There might be something outside worth finding."

Bell and I went out the door, turned right, and starting walking around the house. When we got to the back, we could see that the house was a little over twenty feet from the cliff. We walked so we were several feet from the edge, and jumped back in shock when a small section of earth broke off.

Then, we noticed something protruding from the piece of earth that had just crumbled away. We cautiously stepped forward. Sticking out of the dirt was a bone.

"Granny!" I yelled.

"Yana! Bell yelled.

Granny came out followed by Tobias.

"Look here!" I was still yelling over the sound of the surf below. "It looks like someone was buried behind this house."

Granny crept near the edge of the cliff to look and made a suggestion that made me a little nervous.

"Charles, take this cloth and grab the bone. See if you can pull it free."

"Uh… Granny, this cliff is crumbling."

"Just use your abilities, Charles, dear. There's no danger."

"Hmm. Yeah. Okay."

I mouthed one of the Romani incantations I learned from Granny's notebooks and reached down and grabbed the bone with her coated cloth.

"Thank you, Charles, dear. Hand it to me and I'll see if I can scry the owner of that bone."

Granny took hold of the bone, and we all followed her to an old stone bench on the back of the house. She sat down. We watched. She started to collapse.

I ran over to catch her before she fell off the bench. "Granny! Are you okay?"

Bell and Tobias also ran over. Bell sat down on one side of Granny; I sat down on the other. We both held on to her. Tobias stood back and watched.

"Charles, what happened? Yana's so powerful I thought nothing could knock her out like that!"

"That's why I'm so concerned, Bell. Let me see if my shamanism will help her."

I held my medicine bag and chanted a healing spell in Ohlone. It took a few minutes, but Granny finally came to. She looked around at the worried faces of me, Bell, and Tobias.

"Ah, dear ones. I'm fine. I'm fine."

"Granny, what happened? What caused you to pass out?"

"The bone. It's not recent. In fact, it is ancient. I think Henry not only kept artifacts from Sutton Hoo, but bones from those burials there. There's a lot of power in that bone. I felt from it that there is more of the body here. It's a shallow grave. We need to find the rest and give the poor soul a decent burial. Charles, you can use your shaman skills to purify the ground for this man."

"I have a folding camping shovel in my Land Rover," Tobias said. "I'll get it. We'll have to be careful digging here. It's very close to the cliff edge."

Tobias retrieved the shovel and started digging right away.

Granny became concerned. "Careful, Tobias. Any remaining bones are barely under the surface."

Sure enough, his shovel hit another bone with his second attempt. He carefully scraped the dirt away exposing a thigh bone. He kept digging further away from the cliff. More bones. More digging.

"Uh… Charles, Bell, Yana. Look here. This isn't the same."

We gazed down into the shallow grave. Part of another leg was exposed. It was newer and still decaying.

Granny crouched down and touched it. "Charles, Bell, dear, come touch it with me." Tobias stood back out of the way. He looked nervous.

As distasteful the idea of touching a decaying body was, Bell and I squatted down across from Granny and reluctantly touched the foot. There was a flash in my eyes, and it happened to Bell too. She gasped.

"Holy crap!" I exclaimed. "Henry Stone!"

Chapter 7

We were shocked. "I assumed those were Henry's ashes in the urn. Who do they belong to?"

Yana and Tobias had the same idea and went in ahead of us while Bell and I stared at the body.

Bell said, "You know, I hope that urn isn't cursed and has been the cause of Thomas and Garrett's deaths. Charles, let's hurry in there and make sure they haven't opened it yet."

We ran around to the front of the house and into the open door. Granny was sitting down with the urn in her lap.

"Uh… Granny, are you sure that thing is safe?"

"Very safe, dear." She opened the lid. "No ashes. Look. It's only full of one-hundred-pound notes. There's probably several thousand pounds in here. Like Garrett told me, Henry Stone had been selling his Sutton Hoo artifacts. He hid his money in this urn. Tobias, dear, drive us back. We'll check into our rooms at the Ship, and you can go on home to your wife."

"Thanks, Yana. You know, the closest bobby is in my village in Saxmundham. Do you want me to contact him about Henry's body?"

"Not yet," Granny said. "There's something terribly wrong about what has been happening here. What we saw of Henry's body looked similar to Thomas's and Garrett's. He might have gone through a forced transference like the others. The police, your bobbies, won't understand. Let us investigate."

"Granny, what about all that money?"

"We'll leave it here for now. Bell, when we go out, use your ability to seal that door. Charles, help me put a spell on the house so no one can bust in to take any of these few remaining pieces or the money. Tobias, can you cover those bodies back up?"

"Aye. Will do."

We all went outside. After Tobias returned, Bell said a few words and the door with no lock locked. Granny and I spoke a few more words, but in Romani, and sealed the house up tight.

"Okay, Tobias, let's head back to town. And thank you for everything."

"You don't have to thank me, dear Yana. It's been great seeing you again."

We all climbed into Tobias's Land Rover. The dirt road we drove along was dry, as if no rain had fallen for weeks, even though it seemed like it had rained when we arrived earlier.

Tobias dropped us off at the Ship Inn and left. After getting settled into our two rooms, we went downstairs to the pub and ordered some lunch. The place was busy with several tourists, and it took a while for us to get our food. The wait was worth it. They served some of the best fish and chips I'd ever tasted. Along with a pint of Tetley's, it was even better.

Because the place was nearly full, we had to talk to each other telepathically. I started. *"As soon as we're finished here, we should go over to the museum..."*

"And?" Bell asked.

"These fish and chips are so good. This cream ale is too." I nodded in the direction of the door. Bell and Granny glanced that way. Ian had come in. No more telepathy. He might catch on to our conversations.

He saw us and came over. "So, how was your exploration of old Stone's home? Find anything of interest?"

Granny answered. "No, Ian. Just a few old knickknacks. Not anything to write home about. We're thinking about going out again in a few minutes to look around some more."

"I would not advise it if I were you. A bad storm is brewing and might cause more of the cliff to go. It could take the house with it."

"I don't think we have to worry about that," Granny said with her eyes squinted at Ian. "We can be careful. Right now, I see blue sky and sun outside."

"Storms can happen here quickly. You should all stay in your rooms. It is much safer here."

"No, Ian." Granny said with rising anger. "We are going. If the weather changes like you say, we'll come right back."

"Okay, then. I warned you. Good day, Ma'am." He actually shook his finger at Granny. With that he left. He still didn't look at me.

"Why did he come in here? Just to tell us to stay away from that house?" I asked.

Bell said, "He didn't come in for lunch, that's for sure. I'm sure he's trying to scare us away."

"He also knows about Tobias," I said. "And he knew

about Henry Stone's abilities and now ours too."

"I'm sure he's aware," Granny said. "Let's head back to the house and see if Ian causes a fake storm to discourage us. If we block it, he'll know for sure. We have to be alert just in case he tries something else."

We paid our tab and walked out the door. We noticed Ian standing by his museum's front door watching us. We turned and started walking toward the house.

No weather changed. We made it to the house. Still sunny, cool, and clear.

Bell used her ability to unlock the door. We went back in to notice someone had already been there. Somehow, they got in through our spells. Granny went right for the burial urn. Empty. The money was gone. I looked at the cabinet. The few remaining artifacts were also gone.

"Was Ian here? Was that why he was warning us off? Uh… Granny, what's wrong?"

"If it was Ian, why didn't he take everything after Henry died? I think we're up against someone, or something else here. Charles, be a dear and go out and check on those graves. Tobias covered them over before we left earlier."

I went out the door and walked to the back of the house. I quickly came back.

"The graves are open, and both bodies are gone."

"Okay, dear ones, let's go back to talk to Ian. Time to find out if he's been up to this."

Twenty minutes later, we were walking up the steps to the museum. I started to open the door, but it was locked.

"I'm sure he's in there," I muttered. "Bell, how about unlocking the door for us?"

She started to use her unlocking incantation and the door opened.

"That was quick," I said.

"That's because I never finished saying the words. The door opened by itself."

"No, it did not. I opened it." Ian seemed to have appeared out of nowhere and was now standing in the doorway glaring at us. "Now, why are you here? I have closed for the rest of the day! I have a lot of work to do! Please go!"

He started to close the door, but Granny put her hand up and the door couldn't close. She walked in. Bell and I followed.

"Now wait a minute! I told you I'm closed! You cannot just march in here uninvited! Get out! Get out!" Ian was flustered and his wrinkled skin was turning red. I was watching him carefully just in case he tried to cast a spell on us. He was barely an inch or two taller than Granny and was looking straight into her eyes. He still avoided looking at me. Time to assert myself. I stepped between Granny and Ian and forced him to look at me directly. I was holding my medicine bag, mainly to avoid another headache I thought would happen. However, my hand on the bag tingled, and I imagined seeing my grandfather, Peter Red Feather, again. I was surprised at the result.

Ian took a calming breath, went to his chair behind the gift shop sales counter and sat down with a thud. "I am so sorry. I know who you are, Mister Blue. I was afraid you might cast a spell on me."

"Why would you think that? I don't deal in black spells. We just want to talk to you."

"I know you can look into people's eyes to know about them or if they tell truth or lies. I worried you would find out about me."

"I have looked into your eyes. But, no, I could see nothing.

Uh... what?" Granny grabbed my arm.

"Charles, dear, why don't you and Bell go wait for me at the pub. I will talk to Ian privately. Yes, dear, I'll be okay. My old fortune-telling mind can finally see that Ian is not a threat to us at all."

Reluctantly, Bell and I walked out of the museum and went next door to The Ship. We sat down in one of the wooden booths and decided to order a couple of drinks. Bell got a glass of white wine, an imported German reisling, I got a glass of red, French, from Provence.

"Bell, what do you think Granny is up to? Suddenly she doesn't seem to think Ian is the perpetrator of all that's been going on around here. I'm just not sure."

"I don't know either. I really worry about Yana when she wants to do things on her own. She gets so tired sometimes. I know it's your medicine bag that helps her keep going."

"Yeah, I worry too. I've had to use it several times lately when she gets winded walking with us. Hmm. Say, this is good wine. Want a taste?"

We swapped glasses and tried each wine. Bell smacked her lips. "That is good. Maybe when this investigation is over, we can take a little trip to Provence and try some other wines there."

"How about some wine for us too?" Granny and Ian were standing by our table. Bell got up and sat by me, letting Granny and Ian sit across from us. They were both smiling.

"Uh… what would you both like?"

"Same thing you and Bell are drinking. White for me, red for Ian. Right Ian?"

"That would be wonderful, Yana."

Bell let me get up to order the drinks. I kept glancing back at the table in bewilderment. Granny and Ian were talking and laughing. I was very curious why his attitude changed so drastically. Then I remembered what Tobias told us—Ian blew hot and cold.

I didn't know if Ian could speak telepathically, so I thought I'd test him out. *"Ian, do you want a French or German red?"*

No answer from him, but from Granny. *"He'll take the French, dear Charles. Ian's gotten a little hard of hearing telepathically. He can barely hear me."*

I brought the wine glasses over and sat down next to Bell. I asked Ian out loud, "So, how long have you been running the museum?"

"I have not been keeping track of the number of years, but it has been a very long time. Now, I have a question for you. How did you calm me down? Some warlock spell?"

He said that a little too loud, and a few heads at the other tables turned to look at us. I tried telepathy again. *"Ian, can you hear my voice in your head?"*

He spoke out loud. "Are you trying to contact me? I can barely hear you."

Granny reached over and touched Ian on the arm and said telepathically, *"Ian, dear, put your hand out and let Charles touch it. Don't worry, there's no danger. Charles is very gifted, and we need to discuss things telepathically so no one else in here can listen."*

Ian laid his right hand on the table in front of me. I reached out to touch it, and he started to pull it back. Granny again told him not to worry. He extended his hand again, and I laid my hand on his. *"Now can you hear me? Answer in your mind."*

"Incredible. I can hear you quite well now. So, I'll ask again. How did you calm me?"

"See this medicine bag around my neck? It belonged to my grandfather, who was an Ohlone Indian shaman. I not only have the warlock abilities from Granny's Roma background, but also shamanism from my grandfather."

"I know what a shaman is, but what is an Ohlone Indian?"

"The Ohlone are American Indians who lived on the Central California coast for centuries. Many died from diseases brought in by the Spanish soldiers and missionaries, and more died as slaves for the same people. There are mass unmarked Indian graves by several of the old California missions I visited with my... parents. Fortunately, my grandfather's ancestors survived and were able to avoid the Spaniards. Anyway, an Ohlone shaman could bless the earth, heal wounds and minds, and ease anxiety and anger. When I eased your mind, I spoke in my own mind one of the Ohlone healing rituals. Do you understand?"

"I think so. That is a lot to take in. I only know what I heard about you from Tobias. He made you sound dangerous to me. I see now that is not true."

Granny cut in but spoke out loud. "Let's finish our wine and go back to the museum where we can talk more." Then she said telepathically to me, *"We need to find out what has been going on at Henry Stone's place."* And, she thought to herself, *"And find out why Tobias told Ian that Charles is dangerous."*

Ten minutes later we were all back at the museum. Ian wanted to give us a little background on himself, and he had some items he wanted to show us. And they were not reproductions.

Chapter 8

Ian began his story.

"Over fifty years ago, I was, like my old friend Henry, a digger on the Sutton Hoo archeological site. Basil Brown, the amateur astronomer and archeologist, hired us and some locals to help dig through the burial mounds. We had to work fast, as war with Germany was imminent. After we unearthed the ship burial, which was totally missed by early plunderers, we discovered a wealth of artifacts. Other burial mounds still held some treasures, but many had been looted. Several of us, including Henry and myself, pocketed many pieces for ourselves. We figured we were owed them, since Basil kept so busy and was so absentminded, he would forget to pay us. Half the artifacts we would take, half we would hand off to the British Museum archeologists to study. Many of those are in the British Museum. The ones you saw there."

I had to ask. "Your exhibits here are all reproductions. Are you saying you have the originals stored somewhere?"

"Yes, I do. I must admit I have twenty of the original

Sutton Hoo artifacts in hiding here. Henry had nearly the same number but sold most of his."

Bell asked, "Why did you take the pieces? Did you plan to sell them too?"

"Well, yes and no. We planned on selling them originally to supplement our meager income, but the war happened, so I never got around to it. I think Henry sold most of his before he died. He was broke and was selling his pieces to pay for his... uh... problem. Yes, Henry had a gambling problem. He was constantly betting on sporting events and got so in debt, he ended up borrowing quite a bit of money from... I think you call them loan sharks. It was a bookie in Ipswich. He was not a nice man. Henry got roughed up by two of his collectors. Henry was in bad shape after he was attacked, and I am sure that weakened him and his powers. I stopped in to see him about a week after the attack and he was not there. I thought he had gone somewhere safe to recuperate. I had no idea Henry was... dead."

"But who notified Garrett and Thomas about his death?" I asked. "If you didn't know Henry was dead, who knew it and arranged the lawyer... oh yeah, solicitor, to contact Thomas. Jeez, Henry's body was hidden in a shallow grave by someone. How could a solicitor know of his death and to contact Thomas so soon?"

"Yes. I do remember young Mister Stone coming in here," Ian said. "I never saw him again."

I continued. "Also, Garrett had no idea Thomas was here. He arrived here before Garrett, who came to England to move into his new home in Southwold. That's why he sold Granny his house in San Francisco. Garrett was notified while here by Henry's so-called solicitor of Henry's death. Garrett was told to scatter Henry's ashes in the ocean as per his wishes. Now we know that's not true."

We were all silent for nearly a minute, trying to think of why Garrett and Thomas were told to come here and by whom.

Granny finally spoke. "Ian, have you ever noticed that any of the artifacts you and Henry picked up had certain… unusual traits?"

"Well, none of mine, but… I am afraid several that Henry took from the body in the ship burial did have some kind of power. Especially an unusual ring, much like that one on your finger, Mister Blue." Bell held out her hand. "My goodness. You have one too. They look identical to the one at the British Museum. You both saw that ring. That and Thomas's severed finger had somehow appeared in the display case."

Ian thought of something else. "Oh, and one other thing. Back during the Sutton Hoo digs, Henry fell in love with Edith Pretty even though she was a few years older than he. She owned the Sutton Hoo land. She had one child, Robert, by her husband, who was a real archeologist and Egyptologist. He died years before. Unfortunately, Edith died a few years later. Henry took in Robert and raised him as Robert Stone, who, when older, married an American woman and moved to San Francisco. Their only child was Thomas."

"What a minute. Henry had abilities. Did Thomas and his father know about it? We had to lighten the protection spell to get in."

Granny commented, "Well, maybe Henry's spell allowed family to enter. Unfortunately, both of them have… gone on to the great beyond. And we know Garrett had very strong powers… like mine. He should have been aware of the house's strong protection spell. Also, he shouldn't have been transported to San Francisco so violently. He could have protected himself. I'm not sure about Thomas though. Remember, when I touched the house, I mentioned there were others in the past who disappeared the same way."

"That should be in police records as missing persons, you'd think," I commented.

"Our one constable in the area is not too keen on taking notes. He is… how should I say this… one brick shy of a full load. He really needs to retire."

"Okay," I cut in. "What about these artifacts you were going to show us?"

"Oh yes. Please follow me."

Ian walked over to a massive dark oak bookcase, touched a waist-high shelf, said a few words, and the cabinet slid to one side exposing a doorway that led into a narrow room. There were no windows, only a pair of vents in the ceiling to regulate the temperature and humidity. After we entered, the cabinet on the museum side slid closed.

Along the back wall were two six-foot-high glass front cabinets. Each of the cabinet's double oak and glass doors were locked with small brass hasps and padlocks. I was staring in the glass and didn't see anything inside the cabinets. Ian pulled a set of keys out of his pants pocket and began unlocking them.

Once he opened one door, we could see there were quite a few items in there. Ian obviously put a visual protection spell on his cabinets in case someone somehow broke in.

When he opened all the cabinets, he exposed a wealth of 7th and 8th century artifacts. Most were partial pieces of pottery, glass, jewelry, and what looked like a stringed musical instrument. The rest were complete, including a gold buckle, more jewelry, bracelets and rings, a knife with a six-inch blade and highly decorated handle, and a clay flute. There were well over twenty pieces there.

"That's an incredible collection, Ian," I said. "I can see you must have made molds from these for your museum exhibits."

"I did. I did not dare display the originals. If the government knew about these, they would contact the British Museum who would have first rights to this collection. Unfortunately, because the British Museum funded the Sutton Hoo digs, they would confiscate everything without paying me. That is why I made the reproductions. I have had people from the British Museum show up to look at my exhibits thinking I was showing original pieces. I made sure my reproductions had small errors so the museum officials could tell right away they were fakes. They haven't been back in ten years."

Granny said, "Your secret is safe with us. We've seen enough, Ian. Go ahead and lock the cabinets. Uh… does everyone hear that?"

"Sounds like footsteps outside this door," I whispered. "Ian, wasn't the front door locked?"

"I did lock it. Also, it automatically locks if I am not in the main room. Part of my building protection spell. No one could get in unless they are like us. There is only one other living person in the area who has powers."

Granny, Bell, and I said at once, "Tobias."

I was starting to feel claustrophobic in the long, narrow room. "If Tobias is in there, he probably senses where we are. Ian, have you ever shown Tobias this room and collection?"

"No. You are the first. I feel I can trust you three now. I

have never been sure about my… about Tobias. Less now that I know he made up stories about you, Charles."

Granny came over and touched Ian's arm. She spoke telepathically, loud enough for all of us to hear. *"I do sense someone in there, maybe Tobias, maybe not. If it is someone else with powers who we don't know, that might be a problem."*

Bell hadn't said a word. She walked over to the doorway and put her hand on the back of the sliding cabinet. She closed her eyes. When she opened them again, she quietly spoke, "There is someone there, Yana, and it is not Tobias. It is an elderly woman."

"Bell, dear, what did you just do? You could see out there? You have learned more these last few years than either me or your mother could have ever taught you."

"I wasn't taught. I just knew I could do that."

I touched Bell's shoulder and smiled at her. "You are so incredible, my love. Uh… so, an elderly woman. I wonder who."

"That I couldn't tell. I get the feeling she knew we were in here though. I also think she knew I was sensing her. That's probably why she left so quickly."

"Ian, do you know of any older women in the area with powers, besides me?"

"Uh, No. Not… locally anyway. I do know of a couple of young sisters who run an herb shop in Southwold. But they have very minimal abilities. There… is no one else."

"Hmm. Well, anyway, I think we can leave now. Charles, Bell, dear ones. Let's go back to Henry's home so I can see if we can find something for me to scry with. We need to find out more of what has been going on at that house."

"Do you mind if I come along this time?"

"Of course, Ian. Yes, we can probably use your help."

We left Ian's secret room and headed for the front door. Bell asked the rest of us to stand back and wait. She stood to one side of the front door, touched the door frame, and closed her eyes again. She was mentally scanning the street.

"No one out there except a family walking by. We can go now."

My stomach growled. "Say, are any of you as hungry as I am? We should get some food before heading back to the house. Granny, you can't scry on an empty stomach."

"Silly boy." Granny gave me a light slug on my arm. "Okay. Let's go next door and eat. Come join us, Ian?"

"I will be over in a few minutes. I want to check around to make sure whoever was here did not take anything. I should not be more than ten minutes."

Granny, Bell, and I left the museum and walked next door to The Ship. A bus load of tourists, at least twenty of them, had pulled up and beat us inside. We were lucky that we were able to get a table.

"I hope we don't have to wait long to order," I said. "I'm starved."

Granny closed her eyes and mumbled something. The waitress came right over and handed us menus before waiting on the others.

"Granny, I should have thought of that." We chuckled.

Less than five minutes later, the waitress came over to take our orders.

"We might as well order," Granny said. Ian can order when he gets here. It's been almost ten minutes. He should be here any minute."

Granny ordered a cheese sandwich and water, Bell ordered a shrimp salad and got a small bottle of orange juice, and I ordered fish and chips again but with a shandy, a tasty lager mixed with ginger beer. We got our food within ten minutes. I noticed a few of the tourists were a little upset we got served before them.

"Notice that American couple over there," I said telepathically. *"Bell, Granny, they are really giving us the evil eye. And they are not being very nice to that poor waitress. She's working alone and awfully hard and all they can do is complain."*

"Then let's make sure they give her a good tip," Bell suggested.

Granny had finished her sandwich, then said out loud, "I'm worried, it's been a half hour and Ian hasn't shown up yet. I hope there's not a problem at his museum. If he's not here when you two finish eating, we better go back and see what's taking him so long."

Granny got Bell and I thinking something might be wrong too, so we ate quickly. Bell paid for our meals, and we got ready to head back to the museum.

But first, I tapped Granny on the shoulder and nodded to the complaining couple. Granny again mumbled something, and we saw the couple set two twenty-pound notes under their plates.

"Our work here is done," Granny laughed.

Our cheerfulness was short lived. The front door to the museum was open. We walked in and saw that the sliding cabinet was moved, and Ian's secret room was open. We ran into the room and found Ian laying on the floor in a pool of blood. The cabinets that held his Sutton Hoo collection were all opened, and the glass fronts broken. Part of the collection was still there but most pieces were missing.

Bell broke the silence. "I'll call for an ambulance. Ian just moved. He's still alive."

Bell ran into the museum office and picked up the phone.

Dead. The line to the wall was cut. She ran back to the room. "Ian's phone has been sabotaged. I'll run next door to the pub and call."

Ian was trying to move but couldn't. Granny sat down by him and held his hand. "Charles, hold his other hand and use your medicine bag. Quick. Comfort him."

I held Ian's other hand with my right and grabbed my medicine bag with my left. Again, the vision of my grandfather, Peter Red Feather, appeared. I spoke, and kept repeating, an Ohlone healing prayer. I was beginning to worry it was not working, and it seemed Ian had passed out. Then I realized that being unconscious would allow him to be transported to a hospital without pain. Also, my comforting him stopped the blood lose from his head wound. He had been hit very hard, and I worried his skull might be broken.

I let go of Ian's hand, but Granny kept holding on. Bell returned.

"The ambulance is on its way. It may be a half hour, they're coming from Southwold, but the nearest hospital is nearly an hour away in Ipswich. Uh… is Ian…"

"Ian will be okay. Charles comforted him using his grandfather's spirit. Charles, dear, you should go with Ian in the ambulance in case he needs more comforting. It's going to be a long trip for him."

The three of us sat on the floor in silence by Ian. Whoever did this must have taken the weapon with them. I wondered how Ian had been overtaken. Was it someone he knew? And how did the attacker know about his secret room collection?

With these questions running through my head, I didn't notice the sound outside.

"What is that?" Bell asked. "It sounds like a helicopter. It's getting close." Bell ran outside, then ran back. "The ambulance must have been in the area. It's here already. And it looks like a medical helicopter is landing in the field across the road. I'll send the ambulance people in."

Within ten minutes, the medical team had Ian strapped to a gurney and carried him to the ambulance. They told us they would transport him to the helicopter, which would fly to the closest trauma center in Ipswich, about a fifteen-minute flight. I asked the helicopter medical team if I could go with Ian, and they said no… at first. I mumbled a few words, just like Granny would do, and they told me to get in. I strapped myself into a seat, and one of them gave me a set of headphones with an attached microphone to put on. The helicopter lifted off.

I was sitting in the back of the helicopter facing Ian's covered feet. I kept one hand on his foot, and the other on my medicine bag. I kept reciting Ohlone healing spells the whole trip to the hospital.

Another ambulance was waiting by the helipad not far from the hospital in Ipswich. After the medical techs transferred Ian to the ambulance, it was barely a five-minute journey to the hospital's emergency room.

Once Ian was on the gurney and being rushed into emergency, I could go no further with him. I talked to the receptionist, giving her what little information I knew about Ian, then sat down in the waiting room to wait for updates.

I was still holding on to my medicine bag and praying in Ohlone with my eyes closed, then felt someone sit down next to me.

"Not much more you can do for Ian right now, grandson."

I opened my eyes in shock. I felt my heart stop. Time

stopped.

"Grandfather! How… what…"

"Breathe easy, my young shaman. We only have a short time to talk. Time is standing still for everyone else."

"Why are you here in England, Grandfather?"

"You carry my spirit with you and within you. Through your medicine bag, which you use so well, I am part of you. Now, your friend will survive. Your quick use of your abilities kept him from succumbing from his injury. He has good magic within him and will heal quickly. But I feel there are dark forces involved here. I cannot feel who is at the center of it, so be very cautious, dear grandson."

"I will, Grandfather. Whoever is causing so much trouble will not stop at just black spells, they are causing physical harm too. Someone hit Ian on the head awfully hard. I'm sure this someone wanted to kill him."

"And, grandson, he would have died if you were not there in time to recite the healing spell."

"I'm hoping that between Bell, Granny, and I, we can find who is doing this."

"I am sure you will. Ah. My time has run out for now. Your time must start again. Goodbye once more, grandson."

Time started again, and Peter Red Feather was gone. In his place a bobby, an Ipswich policeman, sat down next to me. He removed his hat and pulled a notepad out of his pocket. He had very short blond hair and a pencil thin blond mustache you could barely see. His thin baby face showed he had to be in his twenties.

"You're Charles Blue?" His voice was high, like it never changed during puberty. I nodded yes. "I've been sent to get information on the attack on Mister Malcolm."

"Really? How did you know he was attacked?"

"The ambulances and helicopter must report who they pick up and why. If they pick up someone who has been injured in suspicious ways, police are notified. Anyway, what can you tell me about the attack?"

"All we know…"

"We?"

"My grandmother and my girlfriend."

"Names?"

"Sorry. My grandmother is Yana Blue. That's Y A N A. My girlfriend is Angelina Beltane. Okay, that's spelled B E L T A N E. Anyway, the three of us were next door to the Dunwich museum at a pub having dinner. Ian was supposed to meet us there, but never came."

I related the rest of the story but left out the healing spell part of it.

"Thank you, Mister Blue. If we need to talk to you again, where can we reach you?"

"I soon as I find out if Ian is okay, I plan to go back to Dunwich. We are staying at The Ship Inn there."

The young bobby put his hat back on and started to leave. He turned around. "I hope and pray Mister Malcolm will be okay."

I thanked him, and he left.

I knew it would be a while before I would find out how Ian was doing, so I got up and walked down the hall to a small snack room. There were vending machines along one wall and a half dozen tables around the room. One machine had candy, one had sodas and water, one had coffee and tea, and a refrigerated one had sandwiches and pastries in plastic containers. They had both coin and bill slots.

I reached in my back pocket for my wallet. Not there. Then I realized I had left it in our room in Dunwich. I pulled change out of my pocket then put it back in. I decided I'd better keep it for a Taxi. Hmm. I had an idea. I looked around and no one else was in the snack room. I didn't hear anyone nearby. I put my hand on the refrigerated vending machine, mouthed a couple of words in Romani, pushed a couple of buttons, and a small sweet roll dropped down. I pulled it out and sat it on a table. I then went over to the coffee and tea machine and did the same, getting a black coffee. I hated cheating like that.

Back in the waiting room, I dozed off only to be awakened by a nurse.

"Mister Blue? Mister Malcolm is out of surgery and was asking for you. Please follow me."

It took me a few seconds to wake up enough to realize what she had said. I jumped out of the chair and followed the nurse down the hall. She opened a door to a private room. A doctor was standing at the foot of Ian's bed looking at a clipboard full of papers.

"Mister Blue, I presume. I'm Doctor Hopkins." He sat the clipboard down and we shook hands. The doctor looked my age, or maybe a little older. His short hair under his scrubs hat was almost all grey. He was clean shaven but had very bushy eyebrows. He was the same height as me, but heavier. Looking in his eyes, I saw that he loved good, rich foods. He continued, "I'm the surgeon who worked on Mister Malcolm. He is very fortunate you acted fast to get him here. He has a concussion, and a large laceration I stitched up. It is fortunate his skull was not fractured. I am amazed how quickly he came out of anesthesia and regained consciousness."

"Ch... Charles," Ian spoke, his voice barely above a whisper and raspy. "Thank... thank you."

"Mister Malcolm. Please don't exert yourself. You've just been in surgery and need rest. Mister Blue, let's go into the hall and talk."

I wanted to stay in the room with Ian and use my medicine bag to help him rest. I could tell by his tight eyes that his head was throbbing. If the doctor wouldn't let me sit with him, I might have to cast a little spell so I could. I followed the doctor into the hall. He closed the door to Ian's room.

"Mister Blue, do you know what Mister Malcolm was hit with? It must have been something very sharp, like an ax maybe. If he had been hit a fraction harder, he wouldn't have survived."

"When we found Ian, there was nothing around that looked like a weapon. The attacker must have taken it with him."

"Him?"

"Or her. We don't know. The only policeman in the area is in Saxmundham, and I heard he would not be very good at investigating an attack like this. Is there anyone around here that's like our FBI?"

"FBI? No. Not really. Well, we have the SIS, Secret Intelligence Service, also called MI6, but their job is more global than local. The larger police units like we have here has detectives who can work on cases like this." The doctor pointed to Ian's door. "I understand that a policeman came in to talk to you. Maybe a detective from their unit will travel to Dunwich to investigate. Maybe. I don't know."

And I don't know if they could fathom what has been happening in Dunwich. Not only Ian's attack, but the disappearance of the bodies and the mysterious transference of Thomas and Garrett. "Well, thank you,

Doctor Hopkins, it looks like Ian will recuperate okay. If you need to contact me, I can be reached at The Ship Inn in Dunwich."

With that I left the hospital and caught a cab to the train station and paid the cabby for the short ride with all the change I had in my pocket. It was late, and the ticket office was closed. I looked at the schedule posted on a bulletin board next to the ticket window and saw there was one more train due in an hour. I found a new vending machine built into the wall that dispensed tickets, so, like I did in the hospital, I mouthed a few words and a ticket to Saxmundham printed out. I sat down to wait.

Chapter 9

By the time I got to Saxmundham, it was ten thirty. I had a half mile walk to Tobias's pub from the train stop, and when I arrived, there were still people spread out through the room, probably locals, drinking and talking loudly.

Tobias was not behind the counter. It was a younger guy who looked to be much taller than Tobias's short five foot five. When he stood straight up on the raised area behind the bar, the cap on his head brushed the low ceiling. He had to lean down often to serve the drinks. He looked Nordic and had short blond hair under his hat and was clean shaven. His tight white t-shirt showed off his muscles. He looked more like a body builder than a barman.

I walked up to the bar and sat down there waiting for him to serve me. He was busy talking to a pair of pretty young women who looked like they might be sisters. Both were tall, nearly as tall as me, and had long dark, almost black hair. They were well endowed and wore white t-shirts that showed there were no bras under them. Every man in the bar was staring at the girls. It was hard not to stare.

Finally, the barman worked his way over to me. I first asked if there was a room available. Yes. One left upstairs.

Number 3. I said I'd take it. I then asked where Tobias was. The barman told me that Tobias and his wife left this morning to go on vacation. I then asked if there was any food being served. Kitchen closed. Only store-bought bread and cheese available. I passed on that but got a pint of Tetley's.

The place was noisy. Other than the two women, the place was full of what looked like working class men. Four guys were playing a loud game of darts. Two more were pulling the handles on the two slot machines and swearing loudly at losing each time. I heard them called stupid fruit machines more than once, probably because the reels had cherries, lemons, and oranges on them, and it didn't look like anyone was winning anything.

I drained my ale, then waved the barman over.

"I'd like to settle for the drink and room. And can I get the key to my room please?"

"Just a minute. I'll write it up in a minute." He pulled a cord that rang a loud bell. "LAST CALL!" he yelled.

It took more than a minute. It took fifteen minutes. The 'last call' made nearly every man scramble to the bar for one more round. I noticed one of the women had left and gone upstairs.

I finally got the bill, and then realized I didn't have any money. I hated to cheat again but went ahead and mouthed an incantation making the barman think I paid already. He gave me the key. I was tired and knew I'd be asleep as soon as my head hit the pillow. I went upstairs and unlocked the door to number 3. The room was small, hardly ten-foot square, with only a double bed, a short two-drawer dresser, and one hard wooden pub chair. A narrow double-hung window looked out on the parking lot.

But, before I stripped down to get into bed, I needed to use the bathroom down the hall. I opened the door and promptly ran into one of the young women that had been in the pub earlier. She was wearing a robe that flew open when I bumped into her, exposing all that God had given her.

I apologized while trying not to stare. "I'm so sorry."

"No problem, Mister Blue." She didn't bother pulling her robe closed.

"Uh… beg your pardon, but how did you know my name?"

"My father told me and my sister about you, and, well, about your abilities."

"Your father? Tobias?"

"Well… uh, yes. Mum and dad are… gone. Away on holiday. My sister, Grace, is married to Sven. He's the big guy tending bar downstairs. I came along to keep her company… and have a little fun. My name is Chastity." She smiled coquettishly and winked at me.

I was feeling awfully uncomfortable talking to a pretty naked woman other than Bell, and, with my manhood getting tight in my pants, I was having thoughts of possibly dallying with her. Chastity? She definitely seemed just the opposite. I better be careful. Fooling around with her would be disastrous to my and Bell's relationship. To keep my mind on the straight and narrow, and to keep from staring down at her beautiful body, I tried gazing in her eyes to see if I could tell anything about her. Nothing. I saw nothing there. She must have abilities and be able to block me. I took a deep breath and said, "Okay, Tobias told you about me. Did he tell you about the others who are with me?"

"Oh, he mentioned your grandmother and your girlfriend. I think he said her name is Bell. Cute." She wasn't looking at my eyes as she spoke. Her gaze was at my southern region.

I felt a little tingle on my ring finger. My griffin ring was pinching. My connection to Bell was reminding me to not get carried away. My manhood unmanned itself.

"If you'll pardon me, I'm heading to the bathroom so I can get ready for bed. It's been a very long day for me."

"Are you heading back to Dunwich tomorrow morning?"

"You know about that too? What else did your dad tell you?"

"Uh… that's it. Really," she stammered, which made her look guilty about something, like maybe saying too much. She finally pulled her robe closed and tied the sash. "Well, it was nice talking to you. Maybe we'll see each other again sometime."

She winked at me again, then headed back to her room at the end of the hall.

I had a bad feeling about her. If Tobias had abilities, both of his daughters probably did too. How could three people with abilities in the same family have kept it from their mother all these years? Or maybe Tobias's wife knew and was faking ignorance. Maybe she had powers too. *Hmm.*

I thought about all this while I rinsed my teeth and did my other bathroom duties. When I got into bed, it was as I thought. I was asleep as soon as my head hit the pillow.

I was awakened at 6:30am by a knocking at the door. I got up and slipped my pants on and opened the door. I was surprised to see Tobias. A very tired looking Tobias.

"Tobias! I was told that you and your wife left on holiday yesterday. I didn't expect to see you."

"Eve… she wasn't feeling very well, so we came back

early. We got in at nearly two in the morning. Uh… Eve's got a little fever and staying in bed. Anyway, the reason I knocked is that I'm planning to drive to Dunwich to see Ian. I can drive you there if you want."

"Uh, Tobias, Ian isn't there. He's in a hospital in Ipswich. He was attacked in his museum and left for dead. That's why I'm here at your inn. I helped take Ian to the hospital, and now I'm heading back to Bell and Granny. I was going to take the bus."

"How terrible! Why would someone attack Ian?"

"I don't know. I think the Ipswich police are looking into it. I was interviewed in the hospital, and I think someone might be coming from there to check for fingerprints and maybe find the sharp weapon used to bludgeon Ian."

"This is disturbing. There's never been violence like that in Dunwich for… uh, hundreds of years." Tobias was quiet for several seconds and looked deep in thought. He finally snapped out of it. "I'll drive you to Dunwich, so you won't have to take the crowded and noisy bus. I've already eaten breakfast, so I'll be ready to go as soon as you are. My… daughter Grace and her husband Sven will be working downstairs this morning, fixing breakfasts for all the guests."

"Thanks for the offer. I'll be down shortly."

I hurried. I was eager to get back to Bell and Granny, but I did want to have a decent breakfast first. I ended up eating very little. Two forkfuls of dry scrambled eggs and half a piece of overcooked bacon. I only took one bite out of my slightly burnt toast and washed everything down with a couple of sips of watery coffee. I was feeling anxious and wanted to get going. I trotted up the stairs to my room, again running into Chastity, still exposing herself in an open robe. She winked at me again and started to say something. I said excuse me, edged past her, and entered my room. I put on my jacket and opened my door to leave. Chastity was still there. Naked. Totally. Her robe dropped on the hallway floor behind her.

"Are you sure you want to leave right now?" Chastity came up to me and wrapped her arms around me, pressing her body tightly against mine. She then started to move her pelvis back and forth trying to arouse me. I held onto my medicine bag and said an Ohlone protection spell. It helped keep me down, so to speak.

I unwrapped her arms, reached down and picked up her robe and handed it to her. "Yes, I do want to leave right now. You father is waiting for me downstairs. Goodbye, Chastity. Have a… nice day."

She threw her robe at me, swore, and called me a homo, then stomped back to her room. I let out a sigh and went downstairs.

Tobias had his coat on and was standing by the door. We left the pub, got into his Land Rover, and headed for Dunwich.

During the drive we talked a lot, mostly questioning about the attack, the missing bodies, and the strange happenings to Henry and Thomas Stone. I wanted to ask Tobias about why he told Ian that I was dangerous. I also wanted to ask about his daughters, and if they had abilities, but wasn't sure how to bring it up. We were still talking when we arrived in Dunwich. Tobias pulled up in front of The Ship and we both went in.

"Charles, you go up and see your Bell and Yana. I see someone I know at the counter. I'll be here if you need to head out again to the Stone house."

"Thank you, Tobias." I glanced over at him as he walked over to the bar. He tapped someone on the shoulder and sat on a stool beside them. This person looked short and wore a hooded sweatshirt with the hood up. I couldn't see a face. Kind of odd, I thought. Awfully warm in here for a sweatshirt.

I headed upstairs to my and Bell's room. I unlocked the door and walked in. No Bell. Her suitcase was still sitting by her side of the bed. I got my backpack out of the closet and pulled out my wallet, put it in my back pocket, then went next door to Granny's room. The door was ajar. I went in. No Granny. Maybe they're both out at the Stone house, I figured.

But then I realized Bell usually never made the bed. I always took care of that because I often got up after her. Both beds didn't look like they had been slept in.

I was getting worried and went downstairs. Tobias was sitting alone at the bar. The other person had left. He noticed me standing there and could see my concern. "What's wrong, Charles?"

"Bell and Granny aren't here. I'm going to check next door at the museum. If they aren't there, can you drive me to the Stone house?"

"Yeah. Be glad to."

I ran next door only to find the museum locked. I tried Bell's unlocking incantation, and heard a click, but still couldn't open the door. I was feeling too anxious and didn't recite the spell very well. I took a deep breath, held onto my medicine bag to relax me, and recited it again. The door opened.

No one was in the museum. Ian's secret room was still open, and it was obvious no police had shown up to take fingerprints. A dried blood stain was still on the hardwood floor.

I didn't want to touch anything, so I left. Tobias was at the bottom of the steps in front of the museum.

"Nothing? Come on. Let's go to the Stone house and see if they're there. Don't worry, they've got to be around somewhere."

"I'll be there in a second. I need to relock the door." As I said that, I started to get another headache. Ouch! Medicine bag time again. As I stood there at the nearly closed door waiting for the pain to subside, I started thinking of something Tobias had been saying. Or rather, how he said it.

Tobias got into his Land Rover and started the engine.

The explosion pushed me back into the door, breaking it it open and smashing the old, beveled glass window.

I was stunned and felt blood flowing down my arm. My head still ached. I grabbed my medicine bag, said a few Ohlone words, and got up feeling dizzy but a little better. I looked out the doorway and saw what was left of the Land Rover. It was burning and sending up a dark cloud of smoke into the foggy sky. Where did that thick fog come from so suddenly?

The Ship Inn had the front windows blown in as did the museum. People from the pub were out looking at the fire, and tourists were taking photos. Two of them had sat down on the pub's front steps and had a few cuts on their faces and hands from the flying glass. No one was trying to help them. Like everyone else, they were taking photos, like they weren't hurt.

Several locals, including the Ship's employees, ran out

with fire extinguishers. The fire was put out quickly, then the employees tried to coax the two wounded into the pub to take care of them.

And up the street ran Bell. Granny was far behind, walking slowly and laboriously. She stopped and sat down on the grass by the side of the road.

Bell rushed to my side. "Charles! Are you…"

"I need to help Granny!"

Bell looked back and noticed Granny was now lying down in the grass. We both ran back to her. She was breathing heavily and didn't look well. I sat down beside her and put my hand on her head. I again held onto my medicine bag, closed my eyes, and recited the healing spell.

And once more, Grandfather, Peter Red Feather, was taking over through me. It seemed like it took a while, but in reality, it was only a few seconds. Granny sat up and gave me a big hug. It hurt.

"I'm fine now, dear Charles. What Bell and I have been through was quite draining. And when we heard the explosion, we had the terrible feeling you had left us."

"I would have if I'd been in the car with Tobias."

"Tobias? Oh, no! Dear Tobias is gone too?" I saw tears forming in Granny's eyes. She put her head in her hands and started crying. I started to ease her with one of her own incantations she taught me, but Bell touched me and shook her head.

"Give her a moment, Charles," she whispered. "Now, what happened? How did Tobias's car explode?"

"I have no idea. We just got here. I went up to our room, then Granny's, and saw neither of you had slept here last night. I got worried and went to the museum to see if you'd been there. Tobias was going to drive me to the house to look for you. As I went to relock the museum's door, Tobias started his car and it exploded. Oh crud! His poor wife. She's ill in bed. And his daughters are both there."

"That's terrible. And you could have gotten in the car with him." Bell touched my face tenderly. "And Tobias has daughters?"

"Yeah. Two of them. One is married to a guy named Sven, who was tending the bar while Tobias..." I sighed. "...and his wife went on holiday. The other is, I think, a problem child. I'm pretty sure that she and her sister have abilities."

Granny stopped weeping, cleared her throat, and came over to us.

"Bell... you and I should go... to Saxmundham and tell..." She sighed, "...Tobias's family what happened."

"As soon as I... Uh... Charles, you're bleeding quite a bit. That's a bad cut on your arm. Looks like there's a piece of glass sticking in it. Let me..."

"Ouch!"

"Got it. Now let me..."

"Ouch! Bell, what'd you do?"

"Stopped the bleeding, you old crybaby. Okay, lover, now grab your medicine bag and heal thyself."

And that's what I did. I felt the itch of the deep cut healing, and within five minutes the wound was gone.

Satisfied I was okay, Bell and Granny headed back to The Ship to have some water, then pack a few things for the bus ride to Saxmundham. As soon as they came back downstairs, the bus arrived. We said our goodbyes and they boarded it and left. With all that was going on, I never got a chance to ask them what transpired at the old Henry Stone house.

With the fire out, all the picture taking was over.

However, the cameras got pulled out again when a fire truck and an ambulance arrived. The fire truck was too late to do anything except write up a report. The ambulance had the grisly task of taking whatever was left of Tobias to the morgue. I didn't want to watch, so I went up to my room to clean up. I planned to take a walk down to Henry Stone's house and see if I could see what Granny meant when she said whatever she and Bell did was so draining. I didn't like the sound of that.

I took a quick shower and put on some clean clothes. When I got back downstairs, I noticed a small English Ford police car parked on the sidewalk in front of the pub, effectively blocking the front steps. I climbed over the step's railing and slid around the front of the police car.

Beside the burned-out Land Rover was the local policeman Tobias had told me about. He looked old enough that I thought he probably should have retired years ago. On his head was a shiny billed black hat with a black and white checkered band encircling it. His black uniform seemed too big for him and was pretty wrinkled. A baton club hung from the belt on his baggy trousers. He was walking around the burned-out vehicle taking photos from different angles. He saw me watching him and came over.

"This's ah creme sane," he said with a heavy Scottish accent. I was pretty sure he said, 'this is a crime scene'. He continued warning me. "Ya dina wanna be hare."

"I knew the victim," I told him. "Don't you want to know why he was here?"

"Dona tell ma wha ta de-u, ya noosy Ahmeericun. Move a-loong. Move a-loong." He was waving me away with both hands, which caused him to drop his camera in the bushes in front of the museum. "Nah ya see whut ye made me deu! Ah shood ahrest ye fur thut!" He picked it up and dusted it off. It was fine.

Okay. Looking in his eyes I could see he imagined himself to be a Sherlock Holmes. I could also see he was no more than a puffed up traffic cop. This guy was definitely not any kind of police detective, but he was the only game in town.

I just shook my head and started to walk away just as a flatbed tow truck rolled up. It would take some doing to get all the pieces of the Land Rover on to the truck. The policeman was yelling at the tourists snapping photos of the action the same way he yelled at me. He dropped his camera again. I left.

The quarter mile walk to Henry Stone's house took me by the entrance to the ruins of Greyfriars Monastery. Bell, Granny, and I hadn't been able to visit it yet, so I felt compelled to take a quick look around figuring the trail on the other side would take me back to Henry's house. Entering through the stone arched portal, which was part of the original 14th century wall encircling the grounds, I walked up to the remains of the monastery, passing a couple of grazing sheep and a small horse. A single remaining grotesque over a vaulted window peered down at me. I pictured in my mind how the place must have originally looked like, with statues over every window and gargoyle downspouts on the rooftops.

I walked on toward Greyfriars woods, an overgrown section of land that used to be part of the monastery's property. I opened an old wooden gate and followed the barely maintained trail thinking it could lead me back to the road. Instead, the trail extended only about fifty feet to another fence of barbed wire, and a sign warning of unstable cliffs. Just on the other side of the fence I could see a single stone marking a grave that was very close to the cliff edge. The end of a casket was already protruding through the ground. It didn't look like an old one. I leaned over the fence to get a better view of the writing on the stone. It was a new stone with old-style lettering. I carefully climbed over the fence and squatted down to read it better.

"What the hell!" I exclaimed. "Charles Blue? Is this some sick joke?" My head started aching again, but not like before. I was hit from behind. I felt the earth open as I fell. Darkness enveloped me.

Chapter 10

I don't know how long I was out. I was dreaming where I seemed as young as when I was in college and was walking through my San Francisco neighborhood. I turned a corner and was then in Dunwich, England, where a cliff crumbled under my feet, and I fell, and kept falling. It shocked me awake. I was shocked again to find I was encased in a coffin. This was no dream.

If it was the same coffin I saw partly exposed hanging over the cliff, it would surely fall into the ocean with the next storm, or maybe sooner if someone pushed it. My head ached, not only from the blow on the back of it, but with another migraine behind my eyes.

The coffin was unpadded. I was lying on bare wood. I could breathe, so there was still air in it. And light. Through a small crack between the lid and casket, I could see light. Because of the crack I was getting air. Evidently, whoever hit me didn't want to kill me, at least not yet. Or maybe they wanted me to stay alive to experience the fall that would finally kill me.

Enough thinking. I need to get out!

I pushed the lid hard, but it didn't budge. It was nailed shut.

Okay. Time for incantations.

I put my hand back on the underside of the lid and began reciting in Romani first an unlocking spell, which didn't work, then a strengthening spell, which did start working. I pushed and heard the squeak of nails being pulled. The lid opened a half inch then stopped. I repeated the strengthening spell and pushed again. One inch. One more time. Push. The coffin was barely under only a couple of inches of dirt over my head that fell to the side, and on me, as I opened the lid. The other third of the coffin was now dangling over the cliff.

I gingerly climbed out and crawled away from the cliff back to the fence. I used the fence to pull myself up. Dizzy. I felt the back of my head. A very sore, damp lump. I saw blood on my hand. It must have been the same person who attacked Ian. My migraine still hurt too.

I was still pretty dizzy and sat down on the ground. I felt for my medicine bag. As Granny often says, 'thank the gods and goddesses', it was still there. I grabbed it, closed my eyes, and recited the Ohlone healing spell. Grandfather, Peter Red Feather, appeared sitting cross legged next to me. Time stopped again.

"Ah, my dear grandson. It appears you have been injured. Allow me."

Grandfather's ghostly hand touched my medicine bag, and I felt the air turn cold. I still felt my head was about to explode, but that was short lived. When I looked again, Grandfather was gone. So was my dizziness and headache. I felt my head again, and the lump was gone too.

Okay. Yeah. I'm okay.

I made my way back to the monastery and out the front gate. Shortly, I was back at Henry Stone's old house.

The front door was ajar. I figured that when Bell and Granny heard the explosion, they ran out without closing the door tightly. I went inside and sighed at the mess that was left when all the artifacts, and bodies, disappeared.

And, on the floor by the cabinet was Granny's bottomless carpetbag where she kept her scrying pieces. She must have forgotten it when she and Bell ran out so quickly when Tobias's car exploded.

Out of curiosity, I opened it. If Granny was doing some serious scrying here, that must be why she was so exhausted earlier. Inside were two items wrapped in her coated cheesecloth. I lifted one out and carefully unwrapped it.

A finger. Okay, I immediately knew that it was Thomas Stone's. How did Granny get that? It was in a glass covered case at the British Museum. Did she scry with it? No. It was still wrapped.

I rewrapped the bone and put it back in the satchel. I pulled the other package out and opened it. A ring. The old griffin ring we also saw at the British Museum. How did Granny get them?

"Ouch!" My own griffin ring pinched my finger and began to glow, then the old one in the cheesecloth started glowing too. I wondered if Bell's ring was doing the same thing.

I put my ring finger next to the old ring in the cheesecloth to compare them. What happened next left me exhausted. Both rings flashed so brightly I was momentarily blinded. When I was able to see again, I was no longer in Henry Stone's house. I was somehow transported home in San

Francisco. I collapsed on my sofa trying to catch my breath. I think I dozed off.

I awoke with a start almost a half hour later. Thinking I was still in England, I jumped up and hit my shin on my coffee table. It hurt. I then realized where I was and how tired and thirsty I was. I opened our refrigerator and pulled out a bottle of water. I unscrewed the top and chugged the whole thing. As I did, I noticed my hand holding the bottle looked a little wrinkled. I grabbed a second bottle and did the same. I started feeling better. I drank one more. *Okay, that did it. The wrinkles are gone. My hand looks normal again. Wow! Is this what happened to Thomas and Garrett? And is this how the attacker is getting around?*

I was still awfully tired, so I did my medicine bag thing. I breathed easier.

Then I noticed that I still had the cheesecloth with the old ring in it. It was laying on the sofa where I had passed out. *I wonder if I touched these two rings together again it would take me back to Dunwich. Hmm. First, I should call Patrick and let him know what's going on.*

I picked up my phone and dialed Patrick's number. No answer. I tried calling Castillo at the police station, figuring maybe Patrick was with him. I got a receptionist who asked, "How may I direct your call?"

"Lieutenant Castillo please."

"I'm sorry, sir, but Captain Castillo is out. Can I take a message?"

"No. I'll try again later. Goodbye."

They must both be out investigating the Thomas and Garrett mysteries. Hmm. Captain Castillo now.

I decided to see if I could get back to England. Knowing that the transference would make me thirsty, I stuffed two more bottles of water in my pockets then sat down on the sofa again and opened the cheesecloth holding the old ring. I put my own ring close to it again, and, once more they both glowed. Another flash and loud bang. Another transference.

However, I didn't end up in present-day Dunwich. As soon as my eyes cleared, I saw it looked different. It looked… medieval?

I did end up in Henry Stone's house, but the interior was not the same. The first thing I noticed was the hard-packed earth floor. Very little furniture. A rope bed with a straw-filled bag on it for a mattress, and two more straw-filled bags on the floor. There were two three-legged stools. No table. No kitchen. A small fireplace was at one end of the room with a flat stone in front of it with a rusty looking iron pot sitting on it. The fire had been burning and all that remained were glowing ashes hissing with drops of water dripping down the chimney. I heard rain falling heavily outside.

How could I have time traveled? This happened before in Volcano, but it was Dean who used his wizard abilities to make it happen. Oh yeah. Our rings did glow then too.

I was extremely thirsty again. I pulled one of the water bottles out of my pocket and chugged it. Ah. I think that was enough. I felt another migraine coming on.

Again, I held my medicine bag and recited another Ohlone healing spell. *Ah, better. Now, how did I get here? And, why?*

Curiosity made me open the door. It was not the same door Henry Stone had, but a plain hunk of thick oak that left deep scrape marks on the dirt floor.

Outside, I saw people running. They looked panicked. I

stepped out and was nearly blown down by the wind. It was raining hard. Looking down toward the ocean I was surprised to see a city.

Wiping the water from my eyes, I noticed large waves crashing up over the cliff at the end of the street and against some buildings. I noticed one building was angled. Then I saw it disappear, falling into the sea.

"Oh my gods and goddesses!" I exclaimed out loud, realizing where I was and what was happening.

And as I looked in wonder, a couple, a young man and woman were across from me, somehow appearing out of nowhere. They glanced at me with fear in their eyes, then ran off heading out of town away from the ocean. I didn't recognize the woman, but I recognized the man.

Tobias.

I watched them leave, then became aware others were running by and staring at me.

Time to leave.

A ran through the rain back into future Henry's house, pulled the ring out of my pocket, put my ring next to it.

There was a flash, and I felt my ears pop. *Did I hear thunder?*

I was laying in the middle of a forest. My ears rang and my eyes were slightly blinded by the ring's flash. I rubbed my eyes, stood up and looked down the hill. I saw a very busy archeological dig below. A ship has been exposed. Again, I didn't come back to the same time. Now I was in Sutton Hoo. It was 1939.

I walked down to the site, where I saw a couple of workers carefully digging out the inside of the buried ship.

The vessel's rotting ribs were partially exposed. One of the men who was in the boat's remains looked over and saw me standing there. He walked to the end of the hull and climbed out. He was coming my way.

The man wore a dusty tan wool suit with a matching vest. He had on a white shirt with a black necktie tucked into his vest. He wore a wool flat cap as did most of the workers, who also had on wool suits and ties. Everyone had on what looked like rain boots.

"Who are you, and what are you doing here?" the man said in a posh-sounding English accent.

I had to make up a story on the spot. "Uh… my name is Charles Blue. I'm from San Francisco, in the United States. I heard about this discovery and had to check it out for myself. And you are?"

"Brown. Basil Brown. I'm running this dig. Ah. San Francisco. American. That must be why you aren't dressed properly. I've never seen clothes like yours before. Aren't you cold?"

He made me realize how out of place I must look. My sweatshirt and jeans were probably not seen around England at the time. Fortunately, since I had been in chilly Dunwich, I still had on my denim sherpa-lined jacket. Basil looked at it and had to touch it.

"I guess you aren't cold in that. Interesting." He stood back and looked me over again. "Come over here. You can take a closer look at our find."

He led me to what he called the dig. "This is it. If it wasn't for darling Mrs. Edith Pretty, who owns this land here, this wouldn't have been found at all."

"So, she must have contacted you."

"I am an amateur astronomer and was showing Edith's

young son, Robert, the moon through my telescope one night. Edith just happened to mention something about Robert finding an artifact poking out of the ground by that low mound just over there." He pointed back toward another area where two men were digging. "I have a friend at the British Museum and contacted him. I sent a telegram explaining there seems to be burial mounds here. He asked me to check it out. It didn't take long to find a few more artifacts. I then hired some local men to help dig around. That's when we discovered this larger mound with this ship buried in it. No body has been found in it, yet, but we found something else. Follow me."

Basil seemed really excited about telling me about the dig and his findings. He kept talking about it as we walked to a small house on wheels. It looked like a gypsy wagon. Small windows were on each side to let in some light. A kerosene lamp hung from the ceiling but was not burning. Probably used for working at night. Two tables extended along both side walls. A cot was by the back wall next to a stand that held a bowl and pitcher. Next to those was a shaving kit. A mirror hung on the wall over the pitcher.

Basil pointed to one of the side tables. "Look at these. Some of the other burial mounds have been looted, probably hundreds of years ago, but the ship was never touched. Jewelry. Glassware. Even part of a musical instrument. We're finding more each day the deeper we dig. After I catalog these, they'll all go to Edith's house, then later to the British Museum."

Basil seemed to get more excited the more he talked about the dig and artifacts.

Another man entered the wagon. He had part of a gold bracelet in his hand. He handed it to Basil.

"Ah! Henry! You found the missing piece!" Basil took the piece and set it next to its matching half. Basil looked like he was about to hyperventilate. "This is great, Henry. Thank you. Thank you."

"You're welcome, Mister Brown." Henry left.

Basil kept looking and touching the completed bracelet. It was like he forgot I was there. I spoke up.

"Was that Henry Stone?"

Basil set the bracelet piece down and looked at me curiously. "You know Henry?"

I shouldn't have said that. Now I had to improvise. "I know his brother, Garrett. He told me his brother wrote him about this site," I fibbed. "That made me want to see it."

"Oh. Henry did say his younger brother was in America. That is interesting. Small world, isn't it?"

"It sure is, Mister Brown. Well, I must go. I have a long way to go… to hike." I wanted to get away and try to use the rings again, hopefully to get back to the right time and the right place.

"Glad to meet you Mister Blue." He shook my hand. Then he said, "Don't you have a pack with you?"

Oops. "I'm traveling light. I have water and some nuts. That'll hold me until I get to the next pub."

"Well, go that way. Woodbridge is just over that river. The bridge is less than a mile in that direction." He pointed. "Goodbye, Mister Blue."

"Goodbye, Mister Brown. It was good to meet you." I meant that.

I did head in the direction Basil pointed, but as soon as I was out of sight, I slipped between some trees and pulled out the old ring. Once more I touched the ring with mine. They both glowed, then flashed, blinding me again.

When my eyes cleared, I was back at Henry Stone's house. Whew. Wood floor. *Well, I better look outside and make sure I'm back at the right year. Hey. I don't feel so worn out this time.* I took a quick drink of water, just in case. I was okay. Then I saw it. Granny's satchel. I looked inside. Only the package with the finger.

I went outside and confirmed that the graves were open, and the bodies were gone.

I let out a big sigh. Yes, I was back. Then I heard voices.

It sounded like the voices were close and in the house. I thought I recognized them, but it wasn't Bell or Granny. I didn't know who it could be. I wanted to be careful. Now it sounded like footsteps were outside and heading my way.

Think, Blue!

Ah. The shadow incantation.

I stepped back against the back wall of the house where it was shaded from the sun. A couple of words in Romani, and I would be invisible to whoever walked by.

But no one walked by. And the voices stopped.

I waited nearly ten minutes and hadn't heard a thing, so I unshadowed then slowly and cautiously crept back around to the front of the house. The door was open, but no one was inside. I looked back outside to see if anyone was walking back to the village along the dirt road. *Nothing. No one.*

But wait. Something is different here. The furniture has been moved again.

The cabinet doors were open, and the glass was broken as if the doors were swung open hard. The cushion from the easy chair was on the floor. I picked it up and put it back. The bed's mattress was also cut open. It appeared that someone was looking for something. They must have thought Henry hid things. *I wonder…*

Maybe they're looking for this ring. I pulled the small cheesecloth package out of my pocket. *I think I'd better take Granny's bag to the inn and wait for her and Bell to get back. We'll need to talk.*

Bell and Granny took the last bus back, arriving in Dunwich at 6:30. After they got freshened up, the three of us went downstairs for dinner.

The pub was crowded and noisy, which made it hard to even talk telepathically. We ate quietly, all deep in thought, then went up to Granny's room.

Granny sat on the one chair, Bell and I sat on the edge of the bed.

I asked, "How did Eve and her daughters take the news?"

"We didn't see Eve. We were told she's quite ill," Granny said. "We only saw Grace and her husband, Sven. They took it hard, but said they'd tell Chastity and Eve."

Bell added, "Looking into Sven's eyes I got the feeling he was looking forward to running the pub himself. Grace fixed some food for us, but she can't really cook. She gave us only bread and cheese."

"That's all I was told they had when I was there too," I mused. I stopped talking and thought about Tobias. "I still can't see how Tobias's car got booby trapped so quickly. We were only out of the Land Rover for ten minutes or so."

"Thank the gods and goddesses you weren't in there with him," Granny said. I could see tears forming in her eyes. I wanted to change the topic.

"Now, Granny, Bell, what happened to you at the Stone house before the explosion?" I already had an idea of what happened but wanted to hear it from them.

"Well, dear Charles, you're not going to believe it."

"Try me."

"I wanted to do some scrying around the house. We went in and found the finger bone and ring on the floor in Henry's house. Someone had to have removed it from the British Museum and left it there, probably for us to find. I picked it up with my cloth and tried to scry with the bone but got nothing. The ring was another story." Granny paused and looked concerned. "Bell? Should I go on?"

"Please do, Yana."

"Well. When I started scrying with the ring it started to glow. Bell noticed her ring was glowing too. She put her hand on my shoulder and brought her ring close to the old one. A blinding flash of light hit us. When our eyes adjusted again, we weren't in Henry's house anymore. We time traveled to the dig at Sutton Hoo. I see you looking at me strangely, Charles. Hard to believe, I know. Uh... why are you smiling?"

"It's not hard to believe. The same thing happened to me. You left your satchel at the old house when you and Bell heard the explosion and came running. I looked in it and found that ring. It glowed again and my ring did the same thing. I also traveled to Sutton Hoo in 1939. Did you need water when you got to the dig?"

"We did. There was a water jug in Basil Brown's office trailer. We almost emptied it. We needed more when we got back here."

"Did you make it straight back here from Sutton Hoo?"

"Yes. Didn't you?"

"Actually, my first stop was at home."

"Home?" Granny and Bell both said at once.

"Yeah. I don't know why. I was incredibly thirsty and noticed my skin was wrinkled when I got there. I drank several pints of water that were in the refrigerator. Anyway, while there, I tried to call Patrick, but he wasn't in. I then called Castillo, and he was gone too. I used the rings again and ended up, get this, in Henry's house but in medieval Dunwich during a huge storm. I saw a house fall into the sea. Oh, and I also saw Tobias and a woman appear. No, it wasn't Eve. People started to notice me, so I knew I had to leave quickly. I ran back into Henry's house… future Henry's house and touched rings again. That's when I ended up in Sutton Hoo. Basil Brown was surprised to see me, which means I must have arrived at a time before you two got there."

I had an idea.

"Hey! Do you think someone's traveling from place to place like we did? Even though we all time traveled, my trip from home to here was at the same time. Maybe that's why I didn't hear anyone sneak up behind me and club me over the head."

"What! You were attacked?" cried Granny and Bell.

"And put in a coffin. One that was about ready to fall off a cliff. There was even a tombstone with my name on it."

"Charles. Sweet, dear Charles." Granny got out of her chair and sat beside me with her arm around me. Bell did the same on my other side.

"Whoever hit me must have been the same person that hit Ian. But I think my attacker only wanted to stun me and seal me in the coffin. He, or maybe she… I don't know… seemed to want me alive to maybe experience the fall and my death."

"How did you get out?"

"I used a strengthening spell on myself and was able to move the lid a little, but not enough. I tried a couple more times, and it finally worked. The lid opened and the dirt slid off. It was a very shallow grave. I then healed my sore head."

"I wonder," said Bell as she held my hand, "if that's how Tobias's car got booby trapped. Someone must have appeared out of nowhere and set the bomb. Also, could there be other rings like we have? I mean, I made the two rings Charles and I have, and, somehow, the Sutton Hoo ring is identical. Why?"

"That I cannot say, dear," Granny said. "No telling what the gods and goddesses have planned for us over the years. Or, if there's somehow a connection between us and Sutton Hoo."

"I've never been able to craft anything like our rings again," Bell commented. "I tried, but I was never able to make any others."

"Bell, you know it was your mother who gave me my ring all those years ago when we first met. Then when we found another ring, your ring, in the old Mystic Eye display case. Remember, both the amber pieces glowed when we put our rings close to each other. We even felt some kind of vibration from them. The Sutton Hoo ring must add to ours as a kind of time and place activator. Ours never did that by themselves. Well, I don't think they can. Geez. I wonder if there are other rings out there. Other Sutton Hoo type rings?"

"There's one way to find out, Charles. We could try going back to 1939 again and see what Basil Brown and his crew discovered. If Henry Stone took a ring and other items home, someone else, like Ian, might have done the same thing. As much as I don't really want to time travel again, I do think we should go back and spy on that dig."

Chapter 11

"Granny, do you want to come too?"

"No, dear Charles. That one trip was almost the death of me. I'll stay here and keep a lookout and see if anyone shows up again at Henry's house."

"Remember, Granny, I heard no one coming when I was hit from behind. I think whoever is doing this can appear whenever and wherever they want. I'm sure that's what happened to Ian too. Be very careful."

"I will, dear. I'll sit watching with my back to the wall. Don't worry. I hope you two find something out. Oh. And this is very important: Just observe. Try not to alter history."

I mentally crossed my fingers hoping my interaction with Basil didn't have any long-term impact on history.

I put more bottled water in my backpack, then I put my arm around Bell. She held the Sutton Hoo ring in her left hand. We both extended our right ring fingers to the old ring. The glow started immediately. The flash came barely a second later.

Bell and I appeared behind a burial mound less than fifty yards away from the workers. After our eyes cleared from

130

the flash, we took a few sips of bottled water then walked out and came over to the ship burial where everyone was working. It had been raining and several men were removing the tarps that had protected the dig from the recent rains.

Overseeing the work was a man sitting in a wooden folding chair. Next to him was a small portable table with a drink and a plate of food. A cane leaned against the table. He was overweight but dressed impeccably in a grey wool suit with a coat, vest, and tie. His clothes were clean, which meant he was not doing any manual labor. I was sure his size made it difficult for him to even move. The chair sagged under his weight. He saw us walking over.

"What are you two doing here?" he demanded." You should be down there helping to remove the tarps."

"Pardon us, but we don't work here," I said, then had an idea. Bell knew what I was thinking and nodded her head yes. "We are visitors. Uh… American newspaper reporters from the San Francisco Call Bulletin." I pulled a small notebook and a pen out of my backpack (*hope he doesn't notice it's a modern ball point pen*) and acted like I was ready to take notes. "I'm Charles Blue, and this is uh… this is Miss Beltane. Excuse me, but are you in charge here?"

Thinking he would be featured in an American newspaper lessened his anger. In fact, he smiled and said, "Yes, I am. My name is Phillips. Charles Phillips. I'm chief archeologist with the British Museum. My excavation here is the most important dark age find ever in Great Britain. I'm to make sure the findings are numbered and catalogued properly."

Hmm. I thought. Pretty egotistical fat man. Bell heard my thoughts again and poked me in the ribs. I pretended to take a few notes, then asked, "Did you make the discovery?" I already knew the answer. I wanted to hear what he would say.

"I'm responsible for bringing this discovery to the forefront of archeological science."

Evasive. Okay, try again.

"But did you discover it?"

"Uh…" he stammered. "Missus Pretty knew there were burial mounds here. Her father was an archeologist in Egypt, and she learned how to spot potential sites."

"But who did she originally hire to dig here?"

"Oh… "He had to stop and think. "It was one of those workmen down there." He waved his hand toward the dig in a dismissive manner.

I smiled at Bell. She said, "Say. Isn't that Basil Brown down there? It was reported to our paper that he was the one who discovered the buried ship."

"Uh… well, yes. Uh… that is all for now. I'm very busy."

Yeah. Busy sitting there sipping wine and eating cheese.

"Well, thank you very much Mister Phillips." I put my pen and notebook back in my backpack.

Bell and I walked along the edge of the dig and stopped midway to look at Basil Brown and the three other diggers. One was a younger man with unkempt blond hair sticking out of a light green flat cap, similar to the one Basil wore. He was short, probably five foot four, thin and wiry. He was carrying buckets of dirt and mud to a wooden wheelbarrow at the edge of the dig. Looking closer, we noticed it wasn't a man, but a young woman. When she turned around it was obvious. When the wheelbarrow was full, a boy, who couldn't have been older than sixteen, wheeled it a short distance and dumped it.

I saw Henry Stone again. He looked young, but he did have a bushy black mustache similar to one he had in a photo we saw in his Dunwich house. His short dark hair was under a wide brimmed felt hat. Like the other men, his work clothes were a three-piece wool suit. Another workman nearby looked familiar. I couldn't see him clearly, but I was sure it must be Ian.

We heard a yell down below. Henry had found something. Basil came over all smiles and took it from Henry then walked up to Mister Phillips to show him. As Basil and Phillips were looking over the piece, Bell and I noticed Henry pick up something else and, while the others weren't looking, put it in his pocket. Ian did the same. Ah, I thought, those two are starting to make their own Sutton Hoo collections. Now, I wonder who that other person is down there. Someone tapped me on the shoulder.

Basil Brown.

"Didn't I see you here a few weeks ago?"

"Yes, Mister Brown." Time for the story again. "My partner Miss Beltane and I are with the San Francisco Call Bulletin. We just interviewed Mister Phillips over there and got quite a story from him."

"I'm sure you did. He is pretty self-important and thinks the world should applaud him for his work here."

"We know, for a fact, that you are the discoverer of this amazing ship."

"I can't take all the credit. Dear Missus Pretty knew something was buried here. She hired me to find out what it was."

Bell asked, "How is Missus Pretty doing these days?"

"Why do you ask?" he said pointedly. "Your paper doesn't need to know about her health issues."

We knew from history books that Edith Pretty's health failed steadily from 1939 until she died in 1942 at age 59. Before she passed away, she made sure the British Museum would get all the dig's artifacts and the ones she had in her home.

Basil looked angry. "I must ask you to leave. You have your story. Please go."

"We're sorry to bother you. Thank you, sir. We'll go."

Bell and I walked back the way we came and hid behind a burial mound again. No one was around, so I pulled out the Sutton Hoo ring, Bell and I held hands and placed our own rings next to it. Glow. Flash.

When our vision cleared, we saw that we weren't in Dunwich.

We both exclaimed at once, "Home?"

I swore. "Damn! San Francisco! Not again!"

"This is what happened to you last time?" Bell asked.

"Yeah. And look at the date on the calendar over there. We're in the right time, but the wrong place."

"Well, the last time you were here you were able to jump back to Dunwich, didn't you?"

"Well, sort of. From here I somehow went to medieval Dunwich. I didn't dare stay there, so I tried again to get back to you and Granny. That's when I went to 1939 Sutton Hoo. From there I finally got back to today's Dunwich. Uh... I need to get a drink of water. I feel a little... uh... dry."

"Me too."

We got glasses out of our kitchen cupboard, filled them, and drank thirstily. We felt much better and quite normal after the second glass full.

"Bell, before jumping back to England, let me try calling

Patrick again. I want to let him know why Garrett's and Thomas's bodies were dried up like they were. They probably didn't get the chance to drink water on their jump back to here."

"But Garrett ended up in the water. Wouldn't that have revived him?"

"I don't know. I think Garrett was dead before he hit the water. Maybe that Dunwich sailboat we saw that disappeared had something to do with Garrett's death. You know, Bell, when we get back to Dunwich, let's see if we can locate that sailboat. For now, I want to try to contact Patrick."

I picked up the phone and dialed Patrick's apartment. He picked up on the third ring.

"Patrick? Hi. It's Charles. Yes, Bell and I are here in our Victorian loft. No, we'll be going right back to England shortly. Is it possible for you to come over right away? We have important information about Garrett and Thomas. No, don't bring Castillo. He wouldn't understand. Yeah, it is one of those 'mumbo jumbo' things. Come on over and we'll explain. Okay, see you soon."

When Patrick arrived a half hour later, Bell and I undid our protection spell, and Bell spoke a quick incantation to unlock the gate to our back yard and stairway.

I greeted him at the door "Patrick. It's so good to see you." We shook hands. Bell gave him a hug.

"I've got to tell you, I was surprised to get your call," he said. "I expected you to be gone another week or more."

"Uh... well, we will be once Bell and I make the transference again."

"I beg your pardon?"

Bell continued, "Patrick, Garrett, and Thomas both made

immediate spacial transfers from Dunwich, England, to here in San Francisco. Thomas to his apartment, and Garrett, we think, to the yacht harbor."

"But they were both dead and their bodies looked dried up. What about you? Did you make that spacey trip?"

"That's 'spacial', not spacey," I corrected him. "Yes, we did. In fact, I've done it several times now. Bell and Granny did it once before, and Bell came along this time with me. When I first did it, I needed several glasses of water to clear my head and body. It seems the more we do it, the less water we need to drink."

"Wouldn't Thomas and Garrett also need to drink water when they made the jump from England to here?"

"A long quick jump like that dries you out. It is natural to need a drink of water. Several drinks of water. However, someone, or something got to Thomas and bound him up in his carpet where we found him all shriveled up."

"Hmm. What about Garrett?"

"That was different. I think Garrett was already dead when he ended up in the water at the yacht harbor. I believe he was attacked at his brother's house in Dunwich then sent on his way to San Francisco. I was also attacked back there and confined but was able to escape."

Patrick snapped his fingers. "Oh, I was going to tell you this the next time Yana and I talked on the phone. Garrett's head did show evidence of being hit pretty hard. His skull was cracked. Also, Thomas looked like he had been hit and strangled before being rolled up. Uh... Blue, you were attacked too?"

"I was also hit on the head, but only enough to knock me out. I got put into a coffin. Fortunately, I was able to escape before the coffin fell over a cliff."

"Now I see why you didn't want me to bring Castillo. Yeah. Real mumbo jumbo stuff. So, is it possible for me to make the jump to England too?"

"I doubt it. You see, Bell and I have these rings." We both put our hands forward so Patrick could see them. "Somehow, this ring in my pocket is what makes our tripping back and forth… oh, and make time jumps, possible. This old ring in this wrapper is from the Sutton Hoo excavation and is identical to the ones Bell and I have. It's likely there's others too."

"Crud. Time jumps are a little too hard to believe, even for me. In fact, all this is hard to believe. I can't tell Castillo any of this. I'd be laughed out of San Francisco."

"Well, believe it or not, Bell and I were just in 1939 at the Sutton Hoo ship excavation."

"You've lost me. What is this Sutton Hoot thing?"

Bell replied, "Sutton *Hoo*. It's a place on the east coast of England where there was a buried ship. The British museum says it was a burial for a man of importance back in 600 or 700 AD. It was claimed to be the most important archeological discovery of its time. Many of the artifacts from there are on display in the Museum."

"And you visited this site?"

"Yes, and we saw a young Henry Stone, who was Garrett's brother, pocket some pieces. Probably this ring. Henry had a cabinet with a few remaining artifacts he stole from the site. They were stolen not long after we went to the house. I think someone was looking for this ring Charles has in his pocket. It is incredibly powerful."

"I don't know what to say. Or do. Are you going to go right back to England now?"

"Yeah, Patrick. We've got to get back to Granny. Whoever

is attacking those associated with Henry Stone's house, seems to pop out of nowhere. Granny is aware, but I am worried."

"Can I watch?"

"I'm sorry Patrick, we don't know what might happen to you when you see the flash from the rings. Hopefully, nothing, but we can't take the chance. We're still trying to get used to it. Besides, once you leave, Bell and I must put the house back on protection mode."

"Well, I'm really going to worry about you now that I know what's going on. Next time, take a flight home… all of you. I miss Yana's teachings. I miss you guys. Please be careful."

After hugs all around, he left.

Bell and I reinstated the protection spell and relocked the gate after we heard Patrick's car leave.

"Okay, Bell. You ready?"

"Not really, but we can't stay here." She sighed. "Let's go."

I pulled out the Sutton Hoo ring, and we, once again, put our own rings close to it. Again, glow. Again, flash.

And again, we were not in Dunwich. We were back in Sutton Hoo. But this time, no one was around. The ship was covered over with dirt, and it looked like an unexcavated burial mound again.

Overhead was the thunderous roar of airplanes heading east over the English Channel. World War II was happening.

"Bell, we've got to get out of here! Why did we arrive back here, at this time?"

"Charles, the sky is clouding over. I hear thunder… or maybe explosions. We should go quickly before a storm hits. Who knows what an electrical storm might do to our transference."

"Okay. Let's go again. Think Dunwich, present day."

We did our ring thing again.

Glow. Flash.

Sitting right next to where we reappeared in Stone's house was Granny sitting in a chair. Head bowed, napping.

"Granny!"

"Yana!"

She awoke and smiled at us.

"Ah. Children. Did you have a nice trip?"

"No, Granny. We've traveled all over the place. Sutton Hoo during the dig, then home again in San Francisco, where we were able to contact Patrick. We then tried to come back here but ended up in Sutton Hoo again, but a year or two later when the war was happening. The burial was covered over, and the sky was full of planes heading to Europe. It was scary."

Bell shivered. "I don't want to travel like that anymore. No telling where or when we could end up."

I was thinking I might have to make another jump on my own to find out more, but later. Much later. "So, Granny, did anything odd happen here while we were gone?"

"Nothing. It's been very quiet. I thought I heard someone walking in the gravel out front right after you left, but when I looked, there was no one there. It might have been a dog or some wild animal."

"Well, I'm going outside to check. If it was an animal, there might be footprints."

"I'm going with you, Charles."

Bell and I went out front and looked around for any footprints. Nothing in front. We walked around to the back of the house to check there. And, right under a small window were footprints, and it looked like someone was standing on their toes to peer inside. Bell and I looked at each other and thought the same thing. Maybe Granny could touch the footprint and try to scry where it came from.

As we turned to go back inside, we noticed a boat down at the bottom of the cliff anchored just offshore. It had two masts. It was the same boat we saw in San Francisco. We also saw someone rowing a small inflatable boat out to it. It looked like it might be a woman. She was too far away and was facing away from us and was covered in a hooded raincoat. A bank of fog was coming in.

We ran to tell Granny. She followed us outside and we stood close to the cliff edge looking out to the sea.

The fog was gone. The boat was gone.

"Are you sure you saw the boat out there?"

"Bell and I both saw it," I insisted. "We saw someone, maybe a woman, rowing out there. We couldn't tell who it was."

"Did you see the color of hair?"

"No. They were wearing a hood."

"You're thinking it might have been a woman?"

"It looked like one to us," Bell replied. "How about those footprints under the window? Can you touch those and see who it was?"

"I'm afraid not, dear. I need a solid object to scry with. Footprints don't work."

I had an idea. "Granny, what about that coffin I was forced into? Maybe the carved stone too. The one with my name on it… if it's still there."

"Well, dear, that might work. Where is it?"

"At the end of the trail going toward the cliff behind the

Greyfriars Monastery ruins."

"The sun is about to set, children. It's getting too late to go now. You two have been through a lot today, so let's go back to the inn to eat then get some rest. We can head to the ruins early tomorrow."

Bell and I went to our room right after dinner and, after showering, we were asleep within a half hour. Granny stayed downstairs. She told us, telepathically, that she wanted to keep a look out and listen for anyone who seemed out of the ordinary. I smiled and replied, *"Heh. Besides us?"*

Morning came fast. I had been dreaming of time traveling all the way back to when the Sutton Hoo ship got buried. When I felt myself being buried alive in the ship and began knocking on a coffin lid, I awoke to a real knocking on the door. Bell stirred.

I got out of bed and pulled my pants on and opened the door. It was Granny.

"Hey, you two lazy heads. It's after seven. You've been asleep over nine hours. Get your bodies moving so we can have some breakfast and head over to the ruins."

I closed the door and went over to kiss Bell. She had dozed off again. My kiss woke her, and she smiled up at me then reached up and pull me down on top of her. Oh, how I wanted to make love to her. She was so beautiful when she smiled. *Gee. I say that a lot.*

She heard my thoughts. "Thank you, lover, but we do need to get going. Maybe tonight we could…" She whispered the rest in my ear, which made me start to get an erection. *Ouch. Not good in my jeans with no underwear on.* My sore member faded quickly. "Well, I better get dressed properly."

After breakfast, we began walking to the Greyfriars Monastery ruins.

We got barely a hundred yards when Granny began breathing hard. She grabbed my hand. "It's time… dear… Charles. Do your… shaman thing."

I did, and Granny breathed easier and was able to make it to the ruins.

We headed to the back of the field and to the trail. We followed it to the fence with the 'dangerous cliff no trespassing' sign. Just on the other side was the remnants of the grave. Part of it was open on the cliff. No coffin.

I told Granny and Bell to stay there. I climbed over the fence and carefully looked at a very moss-covered stone. My name wasn't on it. It was the original grave owner's name, with a 1600 date on it. I started to reach toward it.

"Don't touch it!" Granny yelled. "If that was moved when the stone with your name was put in, I might be able to see who moved it. Come back here, Charles, and help me get over this fence."

Bell spoke up. "Yana, let me help. Stand back, please. You too, Charles."

She closed her eyes and spoke a few words I didn't recognize. The section of fence in front of us fell, allowing Granny to walk right up to the stone.

"Bell, love. That was amazing. That was kind of like what a wizardess would do. How did you learn that?"

She shrugged. "I just knew I could do it. Now, Granny, you ready? Charles and I will move away a little and keep quiet."

We did. Granny touched the stone and started her scrying.

Something was happening. I was getting another bad

headache. And right in front of us a glowing male apparition appeared right behind Granny. The light from him blinded us, but I was sure it reached out and touched her shoulder.

And before I could do anything, Granny disappeared, along with the apparition.

Chapter 12

"Granny!" I yelled.

"Yana!" Bell yelled.

We stood there shocked and stared with our mouths open at the spot where Granny was. When I snapped out of it, I fell to my knees in pain and loudly exclaimed, "What the hell was that?"

I quickly took care of my headache with my medicine bag, then got up and both of us jumped over the fallen fence and knelt where Granny had been. The temperature changed drastically at that spot. Very cold.

Her bottomless carpet bag was still next to the stone and open. I looked in to find it empty.

"Bell," I said with a lump in my throat. Tears were forming in my eyes. "We've got to find Granny. She's got to be okay. She's got to be."

Bell's eyes were tearing up too. She asked," Do you think if we both touch this stone that apparition might show up again?"

"I don't know. Let's try it."

I put my arm around Bell, and we reached over and touched the stone.

"I feel nothing happening except for the coldness. Uh... Charles, what's wrong?"

I had closed my eyes. Bell had taken her hand off the stone, but I kept mine on. I was seeing something in my mind. I felt I was scrying. I also felt myself getting very tired. I let go of the stone and collapsed backwards. Bell caught my head before I hit the ground.

Luckily, I didn't pass out. I grabbed my medicine bag again and mumbled a few words in Ohlone. A little better. I was able to sit up.

Bell was very concerned. "Charles. My love. Are you okay?" I nodded yes. "What just happened? Did you scry? Did you see something? Granny?"

"Not Granny, but I did see what we must do. We have to time travel again."

"Oh, God! I was hoping we wouldn't have to do that again!"

"Bell, it could be the only way to get Granny back. Touching that stone showed me that we have to travel a long way back in time. Back to 690 AD. Sutton Hoo."

"You're serious? Really? Sutton Hoo again? Why so far back?"

"That's when this ring in my pocket got buried with its owner. That apparition we saw... did you notice what he was wearing?"

"He didn't look like he was wearing modern clothing, but his glow was blinding and made it hard to see for sure."

"It was leather, probably deer or reindeer, and some kind of fur topcoat. My scrying gave me a clearer image of him. But I don't know who he is or why he took Granny. If he wanted the old Sutton Hoo ring, I'm the one who has that. Jeez. I wonder..."

"If it's a trap? To get you there with the ring?" Bell asked.

"Only one way to find out. I know you're nervous about time traveling, though…I can go by myself if you want to stay here."

Bell shook her head. "I *am* nervous, but I can't let you go alone. Do we do it now here, or later? Don't you think we should take some bottled water with us, just in case?"

"That's a good idea, Bell. I doubt if there is any good water to drink there at that time and place. Let's run back to the inn so I can get my backpack. We can get some bottled water from the pub. Oh, I don't know how long it will take, so we should take some food."

Bell and I quick walked the half mile back to the Ship Inn and Pub. We went upstairs and I picked up my backpack. Then we went back downstairs to purchase three bottles of bottled water (hopefully, one would be for Granny), a small block of English cheddar, and half a baguette that the bar man sliced for us. We fibbed and told him we were going on a picnic.

We headed back to the Greyfriars monastery and took the trail to the gravesite. We again knelt in front of the gravestone.

This time when Bell and I placed our rings next to the one from Sutton Hoo, the glow was more intense.

It seemed like it was taking longer to flash, and I was thinking it wasn't going to work. Then…

The incredibly bright flash also created loud thunder. Not only were our eyes blinded, but our ears hurt from the thunderous crash. I think we both passed out.

When Bell and I opened our eyes and our sight returned, and our ears stopped ringing, we were back at Sutton Hoo.

Only this time, there was no archeological dig. In fact, there were only a few small hills that look like new burial mounds. We had landed on damp tall green grass on a small, forested rise overlooking the future site of 20th century England's greatest archeological discovery. The whole area below was wet and muddy. We shared a bottle of water.

Below us, a half dozen wet, dirty warriors were shoveling dirt and mud. They all wore the same type of clothing we saw on the apparition. I couldn't tell if any of them were our ghost.

Then we noticed another warrior sitting just below us out of sight of the men below. He was looking our way. He smiled and walked up to us. I started to get a headache and took care of it quickly with my medicine bag. He shook my hand, then Bell's. I noticed he had a short sword in a leather sheath on his side.

He spoke to us telepathically. *"Greetings, travelers. You must be Charles Blue and Angelina Beltane. Yes, I know you would rather be called Bell."*

"How did you know?" Bell asked out loud.

"You speak English?" I asked telepathically.

"Our thoughts join in whatever language you speak. I don't understand what she said out loud. Our old Norse language is so much different than that spoken in your time."

"You know our names. What is yours?"

"I am Lars Asulf. I was the leader of those men down there. They are burying my worldly possessions with one of my crew who died of the fever."

Bell glanced at Lars's ring. It was just like the ones we wore, and like the old Sutton Hoo ring in my pocket. She asked, *"Your ring. It is like ours. Is that how you traveled to our time?"*

"I have traveled to many times and places. However, it is only my spirit that makes the time jumps. I can't send my entire body like you two can. At least not yet."

I took the Sutton Hoo ring out of my pocket and showed it to Lars.

"This ring was found on your ship when it was unearthed in the 20th century. Were there more rings made like the one on your finger?"

He stared at our rings for a few seconds before answering, "There are at least three. Two of them were in our family. One is being buried as we speak. It originally belonged to a sister. Unfortunately, she was taken by our enemy." Lars paused. He gave a big sigh. "She took it off when we were attacked and left it hidden in her home. My brother found it and went on to wear it on this expedition. He took it off to bury on that ship. It is that ring you now have." He pointed at my ring.

"Tell me, Lars, did you take my grandmother? Yana Blue?"

"Yes. And she is fine and resting. I gave her water to ease her discomfort from the time jump."

Bell asked, *"If you time jump as a spirit, how did you get her here?"*

"It is quite easy. I inhabited her body and returned her and me here as one."

That sounded very strange, even to me and Bell. Granny would not allow that. Finally, Bell spoke again. *"Have you done that to any other people? Have you brought others here?"*

"There have been a few others throughout the centuries, but I always made sure they returned to their own time. It is not good to change history."

"So, why take my grandmother?"

"I've sensed how powerful a woman she is. I need to learn from

her so I can rid my time and yours of the evil infecting us."

"Evil? Are you talking about the deaths and attacks in our time?"

"Very much so, I'm afraid. It has even happened in my time. Unfortunately, up to now I've not been able to do anything about it. With your grandmother's help..." Lars paused. I got the feeling he was trying to figure out what to say next. *"And now that you two are here, we can work together and finally defeat Ian."*

"Ian? You don't mean Ian Malcolm?"

"No. He goes by Malcolm in your time, but his real name is Asulf. He's my other brother. He has the third ring."

Ian. A time traveler from this time? And how could he be evil? He was attacked himself. There was no way he could have faked his head trauma and all the blood he lost. I knew that my medicine bag and shaman spells were the only things that kept Ian alive when I traveled with him to the hospital. Without me, he would have died. Now I was wondering if Ian's life was still in jeopardy.

My internal questioning ended as Lars kept conversing to us telepathically. He continued, *"Ian's last time travel was to 20th century Dunwich. He has been there decades now. I am sure his museum is a front for his trying to continue traveling through space and time. But he needs our sister's ring for more time travel power, and if he knows you have it, your life could be in danger."*

I couldn't believe Ian would be a threat to me. I was curious about Lars though. There was something about his story that seemed odd to me. It didn't quite ring true. *"Can you take me to my grandmother? If Ian is a threat, we need to get back to our time to confront him. He may be already back at his museum by now."*

"I doubt that. But follow me. I'll take you to Yana. We have to go back this way. We cannot have my crew down there see me or you."

We went into the forest and walked about fifty yards to where Granny was sitting on the trunk of a fallen tree. She looked downcast and tired but was glad to see me and Bell and got up to hug us. As she hugged me, I had an odd feeling. I grabbed my medicine bag and recited an Ohlone healing spell. Granny didn't say anything but seemed to perk up.

Lars asked, *"What did you just do? I've heard of some in my time who have healing powers. You can do that?"*

"My grandfather was an Ohlone… he was an American Indian who was a shaman. I also have the healing and protecting powers of my grandfather." Then I said aloud, "Okay, Granny, are you ready to go back?"

She just nodded her head.

"Are you okay Granny?" *Hmm. Granny seems odd and not looking straight at me. In shock maybe?* Again, that's not like her. I was thinking. *"Okay, Lars. We're going now. You should stand back and turn away. The flash from these rings is awfully bright."*

Bell and I put our arms around Granny, and I took the Sutton Hoo ring, the one that I was told was Lars's and Ian's sister's ring, and Bell and I put our own rings close to it. Just as the flash was building up, I noticed Lars turned back to watch. I swear I saw a small branch in his hand pointing at us. Flash!

All three of us returned to Henry Stone's house in Dunwich. I breathed a sigh of relief that there were no side trips this time.

However, when my eyes focused again after the bright flash, I looked over at Granny, she was laying on the floor. Passed out.

"Granny!" I yelled.

She didn't seem to be breathing. I grabbed my medicine bag and knelt down and recited healing spells. It wasn't working. I tried summoning my grandfather's spirit. No luck. I kept reciting, over and over for more than fifteen minutes. Granny wasn't moving. I started to cry. Bell had knelt beside me, put her arm around me, and laid her head on my shoulder.

"Why? What went wrong with her during the transference? Why didn't Grandfather help? She seemed fine back… what the…?"

Granny's body disappeared. And someone was outside. The door opened.

"Where have you two lovers been hiding? When I finished scrying on the tombstone you had gone. Did you go on another time trip somewhere?"

"Granny!"

"Yana!"

"Why are you so surprised to see me? And why are there tears in your eyes?"

"Granny, we went back to the 7th century to bring you back here. Have you been here all this time?"

"Of course. I've not gone anywhere except back to the inn, where I found that Ian returned and was still very weak. I put him in my room to rest. I was taking care of him then came back here to see if you were back. What's wrong? Why are you crying?"

"Bell and I thought you had been captured by Lars."

"Lars? Who is Lars?"

"He was the leader of the ship buried in Sutton Hoo. He said he was not buried there. It was one of his crewmen. We were sure he took you, and we went to get you back. But you died coming back from the 7th century with us. I tried to use my medicine bag to revive you, but nothing worked. Then you, or it, disappeared."

"That's because it wasn't me. That must have been quite the enchantment someone put on you. If it was just an image of me, your Ohlone healing spell would have no effect."

"Bell, Lars was not honest with us. Do you think he was after our rings?"

"If he was, he could have tried to get them when we were there. Anyway, could he be the attacker? Not Ian as he kept insisting? I know it's hard to believe, especially if he can only travel as a spirit."

"But, Charles, your grandfather, Peter Red Feather, can touch us when he visits you as a spirit."

"That's right! Maybe Lars can do the same? He touched Granny… but it wasn't Granny. What we saw was an image of her being taken. Lars conned us. Maybe Ian is not his brother."

"Charles, Bell, what are you talking about?"

"Lars told us that Ian was his brother. He said that Ian's real last name is Asulf. Not Malcolm. He also said Ian was evil. I can't believe that. Especially after he was attacked so violently."

"Charles, dear, I can't believe that either. I was just with him. He's very weak, but he did tell me how he appreciates all you did to save him."

"Granny let's go back to the inn. If Ian's up to it, I'd like to talk to him about Lars."

Once in the Inn we went upstairs and followed Granny to her room. When she opened the door, we were shocked to see another glowing apparition standing over a sleeping Ian reaching out to him. It looked as if she was about to strangle him.

Bell and I rushed in, yelling at the apparition. Surprised, it turned to look at us, looked frightened, then vanished. A woman.

Our yelling woke Ian with a start. I immediately grabbed my medicine bag and mouthed a calming spell. Ian laid back with a sigh.

"What just happened?" Ian asked. "I had a strange dream someone was attempting to murder me."

Bell told him, "There was an apparition here when we came in. It did look like she was reaching for you."

"She? It was a woman?"

"It looked like an older woman," I said, "maybe Granny's age. But she looked just like a ghost. A glowing ghost. When we yelled at it, she disappeared. Ian, are you okay?"

"I'm okay. I still feel weak, but I'll be fine and back to work soon. Uh… Yana, thank you for putting me up temporarily."

"My pleasure, Ian. Haven't had a man in my bed for over forty years." Granny smiled. Ian laughed, but it made his head hurt. He winced.

Chapter 13

Granny and Ian kept talking small talk. Bell and I got the feeling she would rather us not be there so she could talk more freely, so we said goodbye saying we were going downstairs to have a glass of wine. We also wanted to go over what had happened and try to figure what to do next.

The pub was not busy. There were only two other couples in the place, and they were sitting at the bar. We chose a booth on the other side of the room. Once Bell sat down, I went over to the bar and ordered two glasses of house red, a very dark French wine, that looked like a California Petite Syrah. We both took a sip and knew right away we should have chosen something different. The wine smelled like rotting compost and tasted almost the same. We put the goblets down.

I smiled and critiqued the wine like a Monty Python skit. "Hmm. A bouquet like an aborigine's armpit. A good wine for those keen on regurgitation. A wine to lay down and avoid."

Bell had slept through the years of the Monty Python shows and had never heard their skit on Australian table wines. However, she started laughing so much her eyes were watering.

The levity lasted only a few minutes. We pushed the wine glasses aside and got serious. No one was around, so instead of talking telepathically, we leaned in close and spoke quietly.

"Charles, we know Lars made up that story. But why? Why did he fake Yana's abduction?"

"I don't know. He seemed friendly, but the whole apparition grabbing Granny thing must have been a ruse to get us to ancient Sutton Hoo. And now that I think of it, Lars must have put it in my mind to travel to his time. Remember, I collapsed when I touched the headstone then felt compelled to find Granny."

"Yeah. You knew exactly where and when to go."

"Did you notice he turned to watch us use our rings when we left like he wanted to see how it's done? Who knows. Oh. And did you see what he had in his hand when he turned?"

"I'm not sure. It looked like... Oh my."

"Yeah. I think it looked like a wizard's wand. Maybe that's what he uses to be able to appear out of nowhere. Maybe he's the one who attacked Ian and me."

"I'm not sure what to think. I mean, if he was the attacker, he could have tried to subdue us when we met him. We need to ask Ian if he really is Lars's younger brother, and, if so, what happened to their sister? Remember, Lars said the ring we have was his sister's. Oh..." Bell pointed past me. "Charles, here comes Yana."

Bell got up and sat beside me so Granny could sit across from us.

"Bell, Charles, dear ones, I was just talking to Ian..." She paused. "Uh, you're not drinking your wine. Do you mind if I take a sip?"

"You might reconsider that, Granny. Sniff it first."

"Oh dear. That's pretty bad." She pushed the glass further away. "Anyway, I got an earful of his history. Ian is a really, really old man. He was born in the area now known as Woodbridge but in the 6th century."

"Say what? Granny, that Lars guy said Ian was his brother from Norway."

"You two should hear it from him. Also, we shouldn't leave him alone in case that apparition comes back."

The three of us left the table and headed back upstairs.

Ian was sitting up in the bed reading a magazine. He looked up and smiled at us. "I'm glad you're all here. I've already told Yana a little about me, but I still have a lot to get off my chest."

Then Granny did something that seemed so out of character for her. At least, out of character for what I knew about Granny. She sat down on the bed next to Ian, leaned against the headboard next to him, and held his hand. He put the magazine down, turned, and smiled at Granny. I expected her to say something in Romani to put some spell on him, but she said nothing, except, "Go ahead, Ian, start with who you really are."

I pulled the single chair up on the other side of the bed and Bell and I sat together on it, leaning on the edge of the bed waiting to hear Ian's story.

He began. "As I told Yana, I was born in a village not far from where Woodbridge is today. My father, Arwald, son of Malcolm, known by many as Malcolm the Cruel, was the chief of our village. He ruled with an iron hand and was often brutal in his methods. Also, he claimed he was a shaman. He wasn't. Anyway, my mother was only one of father's many female conquests. When he raided her village far to the north, probably close to here in Dunwich, he and his men captured most of the young women and brought them back. My father went for my mother, not knowing that she had abilities. My mother died when I was not quite seven years old. I believe she died at my father's hand. I remember him angrily calling her a witch several times. After her death, my father insisted on training me to be a warrior like him, which I hated. Whenever I made a mistake, he beat me. Once he nearly killed me when he was trying to train me with a long knife, and I dropped it. I was only twelve."

I could see Ian was tiring, but I was intrigued with his story. I held on to my medicine bag and silently mouthed a healing spell. Ian sighed, caught his second wind, and continued.

"When I turned sixteen, my father loaded me with him and a dozen of his men, with enough provisions for several days, onto a long boat. We rowed down the river, the one called Deben now, then set sail out into the North Sea. Two days later, we raided a coastal village on the south end of Norway. Father and his men killed nearly all the men and took back a few women, along with jewelry looted from the homes. I was sickened by the slaughter. One of the rings father brought back was a dragon ring like those you have on your fingers." He pointed to Bell and me. "Father found out that one of the women he captured was said to be a sister to… well, you know him as Lars. He was the Norse warrior who came back to raid our village. Anyway, she was a very beautiful, young, and powerful witch, and stole back the dragon ring. When father caught her at it and began to beat her, she cast a death spell that finally killed him. I saw this happen and expected her to kill me too. However, she looked at me and smiled. She made me feel free and in love. I helped her escape.

"We traveled together, planning to head north. When we reached Sutton Hoo, we saw no one. All we saw were the burial mounds I much later returned to work on for Basil Brown. But we both felt someone was watching us. Then her ring glowed very brightly, and it flashed, frightening us. Because I was holding her hand, both of us were transported to Dunwich in 1936."

"Is that when you moved into your museum?" I asked.

"Not yet. We also could not speak English yet. With our abilities, we learned quickly. Anyway, she soon gave birth to Grace. But a few months later she disappeared."

"I'm so sorry." Bell said. "What happened to Grace?"

"I was able to find a wetnurse in the area to care for Grace while I searched for my wife." Ian sighed. "It took almost three years, but I finally found her at Sutton Hoo in 1939 when the ship burial was found. She had escaped from her abductor. She gave birth there to Chastity at Edith Pretty's home."

After nearly ten seconds of silence, Bell mentioned, "When we were with Lars, he kept insisting you were his brother. Do you have any idea why he said that?"

Ian's eyes were closing, and he seemed to be weakening again. I thought I would use my medicine bag on him again, but he opened his eyes and sat up a little straighter. "I really don't know why. I've never met this… Lars."

Before Granny or I could respond, Bell said, "You haven't told us her name, Ian. What is her name?"

"Oh. I am sorry I did not mention that. I kept assuming

you all knew. My love's name is Eve."

Eve. Could Tobias's wife be the same Eve? Had she been time traveling? Is that why she was always claiming to be ill and often in bed? Did Tobias know? From what he told me about his wife, I didn't think so, unless Tobias was not telling the truth to protect her. Also, what was Tobias's background? Could he be from Ian's time? After all, Tobias knew Ian well. And Tobias's daughters have the names Ian mentioned? Can all of them be connected to Sutton Hoo?

So many questions running through my head and no answers. Yet.

Bell and I excused ourselves to go for a walk so Ian could get more rest. Granny stayed and kept watch over him in case any spirit or apparition appeared again.

Once we got outside Bell commented, "Ian's Eve can't be Tobias's wife. Why the charade?"

"I was wondering that too. What about Tobias? Could he also be from that early time around Sutton Hoo? And, when Granny knew him, did he just appear in San Francisco? She just said he came from England. You know, because we couldn't see anything in his eyes, we were just taking his word for it. He seemed so sincere."

"It should be easy to check on Eve over in Saxmundham to see if she's there or not. Another question we should be asking ourselves, who killed Tobias and attacked Ian and you? And is that person also responsible for Garrett's and Thomas's deaths? Also, what about that two-masted ship? Both times after we saw it, in San Francisco and Dunwich, it disappeared. In other words, is it real, an illusion, or what? The name we saw on the boat did convince us to come to England. Was that on purpose?"

"Bell, I don't think we'll ever know. Say, why don't we go for a walk along the beach? We can look at the Stone house property from below and see what the cliff looks like under it."

Bell and I made our way down the road from town to the rocky shingle beach. A few other people were sitting in beach chairs just north of us reading books and bundled up for the chilly day. We started walking south.

Walking on a shingle beach was different than walking on the sand of San Francisco and Santa Cruz beaches. Most rocks were small, but several were real ankle twisters. We had to tread carefully. After a couple hundred yards, we reached the area below Henry Stone's house. The cliff rose twenty or more feet above us and was slightly undercut. We looked up just as a section of the top crumbled off. We jumped back as the small pile of dirt fell at our feet.

"Wow, Bell, that was close."

"Did you see anyone up there? I thought I did just before we jumped back."

"I didn't notice. Could you see who it might have been?"

"No. I think I only saw a hand. Uh… Charles, look at that glow. What's in the dirt that fell?"

"Another ring? No. It look's like a small bracelet. It looks familiar."

Still holding Bell's hand, I removed my hand from my medicine bag and picked up the glowing bracelet.

Then a very bright, blinding flash enveloped us.

Chapter 14

We were transported, once again, to Sutton Hoo. Looking around we could see there were no burial mounds anywhere. We had landed on the opposite side of the River Deben, just outside of a small village that must have become Woodbridge maybe 500 years in the future.

Two familiar young men, still in their skinny, lanky teens, were walking toward us.

When they stood in front of us, staring in wonder at us and our clothes, Bell and I both exclaimed, "Ian? Tobias?"

Ian spoke first in a language we didn't understand. I remembered talking to Lars telepathically, so I attempted it again knowing that Tobias in our time could do that. I wasn't sure about young Ian.

"You are Ian, and you are Tobias. We know you…" I paused, wondering if I should say it, then decided to. *"…in the future."*

Tobias caught on quickly. *"Ah. I hear you, and I feel I should know you. Hmm. And your clothes seem familiar too. Now, that does explain a lot. You see, you are not the first to have arrived here from the future. But you are the first to know both of us by name. By what names do you go by and where are you from?"*

"This is Bell, and my name's Charles. We are from a land very far from here."

Young Ian was able to talk to us telepathically. He said, *"There is something about you that is so familiar, even though we've never seen you before."*

Bell asked, *"Ian, is your father, Arwald, still alive?"*

"Why do you ask that. Of course, Arwald, Malcolm the Cruel, our father, is still alive."

"Really? You're both Arwald's sons?" I was surprised.

Tobias spoke. *"Yes, we are. We also have the same mother. If you stay, we must hide you. Our father would kill you outright as witches. Ian and I got our abilities from our mother. Father hates magic and killed our mother two moons ago calling her a witch. He would kill us too if he knew we inherited her magic."*

"We don't plan to stay," I said. "In fact, we should leave now before anyone else sees us."

"Yes, you should," Ian said. *"We will be departing with father soon. He is planning to raid a village in Norseland somewhere. He's been told they have riches far beyond his dreams. My feeling is that no good will come of it. Death and heartache."* Ian looked sad.

Tobias pointed toward a forest. *"You should go there and return to your own time. It would be death if you stayed here. Please go quickly."* As we left, we heard Tobias say, *"Safe journey friends."*

Bell and I hurried toward the forest. Once we were deep amidst the trees and out of view, I realized the bracelet that seemed to have sent us here was not with us. Instead, I pulled the Sutton Hoo ring out of my pocket. Bell and I held on to each other and put our rings next to it. All of them glowed. Another bright flash blinded us.

Bell and I were lying asleep next to each other on the shingle beach below Henry Stone's house. I yawned and woke up then looked around confused. Bell did the same.

"Did we both dream that?" she asked.

"It sure feels like it. But I know we must have traveled back in time and talked to Ian and…" I paused, knowing what had happened to Tobias in our time. "…uh, Tobias. But now I'm not sure. I sure feel tired."

"Me too. You know, I'm sure we saw a glowing bracelet in that pile of dirt that nearly hit us. Look there." Bell pointed at the rubble. "Nothing."

"Huh." I stood up and kicked the dirt to see if anything was there. "Nope. There's nothing here. Bell, hold my hand. I'll use my medicine bag to refresh us so we can get going."

"I'm thirsty. And my stomach is growling. I'm hungry too. What time is it?"

I pulled my coat sleeve up and looked at my wristwatch. "What time did we come down here to the beach? Wasn't it early afternoon? Well, it's now five. No wonder we're hungry and thirsty. We've been here almost five hours." I held my medicine bag and revived us. "Let's head back to The Ship Inn and eat. Then we need to talk to Ian."

A half hour later we were in the pub, sitting in a booth, and looking at the menu. Even though we were hungry, nothing looked especially appetizing. We both ended up sharing a salad and drinking several glasses of water, which we felt we needed after our strange time travel, if that is what it was.

After drinking our third glass of water, we got up and went upstairs to talk to Ian and Granny. I knocked on the door to Granny's room. No answer.

I started to open the door, but it was locked.

"Wha… Bell, can you scan the room to see if they are in there?"

"I was trying to, but my abilities are being blocked. Let me try to unlock the door. Crud. Still blocked."

"Let me try something."

I put both my hands on the door and recited in Romani an anti-blocking incantation I just remembered from Granny's notebooks. "Try it now, Bell."

Click.

"Wow! Charles, that worked!"

I opened the door.

The room was empty. The bed was unmade. Granny's suitcase was still there, but her satchel was gone.

"Maybe they're next door in the museum."

"Or, Charles, they might be at the house. We better go look for them."

"Bell let's freshen up a little first. After our time trip and waking up on the beach, I feel dirty. I'd like to wash up and change my shirt. How about you?"

"Yeah. Me too. I also have a rock in my hiking boots I need to get out."

A half hour later, we were out the front of the pub and headed next door to the museum. The door was open.

"That looks promising," I said. "I hope."

We climbed the thirteen steps and went into the museum. It appeared that someone had been here, but no one was around now. The main room was cleaned and organized. The broken glass in a couple of the cases had been removed.

The large case hiding Ian's secret room was back in place.

"Bell, everything is cleaned up. I'm almost sure it must have been Ian and Granny, but I don't see them anywhere."

"Why don't we check out Ian's room?"

"Let's see. How did Ian open it before. I didn't notice. A button? A lever?"

"How about this."

Bell place one hand on the cabinet and quietly said a short incantation, and the cabinet slid aside.

"Another amazing feat by Miss Bell." She gave me a light punch in the arm. We both smiled at each other, but just for a second.

The secret room had also been cleaned and all the broken glass removed from the now empty cabinets. The bloodstain was gone. We both sighed.

"Well, Bell, it looks like they've been here, but aren't now."

"But why was the museum's front door left open?"

"I really don't know. What I do know is that we should head over to Henry Stone's house and see if they are there."

"I just hope they're okay. Granny tires out so easily now…" I was still wondering how she got around so easily when I was not around.

"Charles let's hurry over there right now before it gets too late. It's after six and the sun will be setting soon. Come on."

Bell started running and took the front stairs down two at a time. I had a hard time keeping up with her. But I did catch up to her and we ran together the quarter mile to Henry Stone's house.

Like the museum, the front door was open. We entered, stood for a few seconds to catch our breaths, then looked around.

"This place is all cleaned up too," Bell said. "Look. Everything is in place."

And like in the museum, the broken glass on Henry's old display cabinet was removed.

"Bell, I don't know if Granny and Ian could have done all this work here and at the museum. I mean, Granny gets winded quickly, and Ian was still recuperating. Where are they?"

"Let's look around the house outside."

When we walked out the door, we agreed to circle around the house separately. Bell turned left. I turned right. We planned to meet in the back.

When we met behind the house, we looked down and noticed footprints in the dirt leading up to the edge of the cliff.

"Bell, look. It looks like part of the cliff was dug into with a shovel. That's what made some of it nearly fall on us."

"I knew I saw someone up there. Hey! Charles! Look over here."

Stuck on a nail protruding from a window frame was a small piece of paper. I started grab it, but Bell stopped me. "Charles. You have some of Yana's coated cloth in your pocket that you keep the Sutton Hoo ring in. You don't need to keep the ring in it anymore. Use that cloth to pick up that paper. You've been able to sort of scry before, maybe you can do it like Yana. Try it."

I stood on the bench and picked the paper off the nail with the cloth.

"Bell, let's go back inside so I can sit down to do this."

"Are you sure? Maybe you should scry right here where you found it."

"Oh. You're probably right. I'll try scrying right here."

I sat down on the stone bench and leaned against the back wall of the house. I took a deep breath, closed my eyes, and touched the paper to my forehead.

Immediately, I envisioned an unfamiliar woman, standing on this bench looking in the window then walking to the cliff where she forced part of the cliff to fall.

Just then my head started splitting again. The pain caused me to lose the vision, and I dropped the cloth and paper as I put both hands up to my head. I collapsed, falling sideways along the wall.

"Charles! Charles! Grab your medicine bag! Grab it!"

Even though I was out like a light, I felt Bell's hand on me. She was trying to place my own hand on my medicine bag. When my hand finally did touch it, I awoke, still in pain, and through gritted teeth I mouthed an Ohlone healing incantation. It was helping, but not enough. I tried it again. A little better, but I still couldn't get up yet. I was having trouble concentrating on my Ohlone phrasing.

Bell had one hand on my head and the other held my hand. I could see her concern. I could also see her saying something, but my ears were ringing, and I couldn't hear her. But whatever she was saying seemed to help me. My headache lessened enough I was able to concentrate better on reciting the healing spell.

I stood up and leaned back against the wall to help support me. Bell was also hanging onto me. I could sense she was worried about me falling down again. I let out a big sigh.

"I'm okay, Bell. Jeez. That was the worst headache yet. It had to be that paper."

"I was so worried. Why… why are you affected so much and not me?"

"I really don't know. Maybe something or someone from the past causes it. Do you remember two years ago after the Pete Ramahi case we were home and our rings started glowing? We felt then someone might have been trying to contact us. Yeah, I don't know."

"We'll find out one of these days. Say, is there something written on that piece of paper?"

"You know, I was so intent on scrying, I didn't look." I picked it up. "There is something here. It's in pencil and a little rubbed off. Let's see. Strange."

"What? What? Don't keep me in suspense."

"It says *'time is on your hands'*. What the hell does that mean?"

"Hmm… Charles, love, think. What makes us time travel? These rings… on our hands. See? But… who wrote that note?"

"It had to be that woman I envisioned."

"Woman? You need to tell me all about your vision."

I told her all about it as we headed back to the Ship Inn hand in hand.

Chapter 15

When we walked into the Inn, we were relieved to see Granny and Ian were there sitting in the same booth we had been in earlier. We sat down with them.

Granny noticed my condition right away. "Charles, dear, what happened? You don't look well."

"I'm just really tired Granny. I was scrying…"

"Scrying? My dear grandson, that is wonderful. But… are you okay?"

"I will be. It really wiped me out. We found a piece of paper behind Stone's house. I picked it up with the piece of your coated cheesecloth I had in my pocket then sat down to scry with it."

I related the vision I had to Granny.

Then I mentioned what happened. "I got a sudden headache, the worst I've had so far, and I blacked out. When I came to, my head was still killing me, and I had trouble reciting the Ohlone healing spell. Bell, here, helped, but it took a lot out of me. I'm still tired. And I'm really thirsty. Let me go get…"

Bell got up. "I'll get you pint of ale. That's what you were going to say. Right?"

I weakly smiled at her and tried to chuckle, but it came out as a wheeze. "Yeah, Bell. That would be great."

Ian put his hand on my shoulder. "Charles, when you are better, I have something important I need to tell you."

"Is it about you and Tobias being brothers?"

"Yes, but how did you know?"

"Let me refresh myself and we can talk. Actually, we'd better talk upstairs. Hey. By the way. You look so much better yourself."

"I do heal quickly. It is because of my… ancestry. Yes, we should talk upstairs when you are ready, Mister Blue."

Bell brought me a pint of cream ale and a glass of a much better French red for herself. I nearly drank the whole pint in one gulp.

"You know, that helped. Now I'm really hungry. I feel like we haven't eaten in days. Why is that I wonder?"

Granny had the answer. "Dear Charles, spacial traveling… well, time traveling too, can really mess up a person's system. Sometimes it is hard to eat. You should go ahead and get some protein inside you."

"Granny, how do you know that? Have you…"

"Oh… I'm so sorry I've never told you before, children. I cannot time travel like you've been doing but was able to do spacial movements. It is getting harder now that I'm older, but I still do it. Well, that's how I showed up… I'm sorry to bring this up again… when your parents were murdered, Charles. I made an immediate transference from San Francisco to find and save you in Sunnyvale. I reversed that transference with you in tow. I knew those who murdered your parents were still there. We had to move fast. I'm sorry I haven't mentioned that before."

Another of Granny's secrets. Maybe as time goes on, she'll

tell me more. That must be how she got around when I wasn't around to help her. My mind was trying to take that all in, but after what we had been through, I shook it off, sighed, and said, "Granny. No worries. As you've told me before, that was then, this is now. I love you, and I'm very glad you protected me and took me in. Now, it's up to me... and Bell... to protect all of you from whatever is happening in the past and in our present."

After sating ourselves with fish and chips, we retreated to Granny's room to talk. Granny was sitting on the edge of the bed and Ian was in the single chair. Bell and I sat on the foot of the bed across from Ian.

Ian spoke first. "Mister Blue, Charles, how did you know that Tobias and I were brothers?"

I related what happened to Bell and me on the beach, and our dream or time travel to the seventh century. Bell filled in the part about meeting Ian and Tobias as teenagers. Ian was completely silent while Bell and I talked.

When we finished, Ian snapped his finger and said, "Now I remember. So that was you. It is no wonder I was afraid of you when we first met. You looked familiar and I couldn't place you. Tobias couldn't either and warned me to be careful. That was... so long ago. I was worried you were with the evil one that plagued me and Tobias. Tobias became too complacent, and that was his undoing. I kept on my guard, but not enough. Someone came out of nowhere behind me and hit me hard. I'm so glad you found me in time."

"So are we. But... evil one?" I asked. "That's what Lars said you were. Is it someone from your distant past?"

"I really don't know. Maybe someone survived back then,

and time traveled like I did. Whoever it is nearly finished me off. Oh… you probably want to know what happened to Eve?"

"Tobias's wife?" Bell asked. "Is she the Eve you spoke of? When Yana and I went to tell her and her daughters what happened to Tobias, the one daughter, Grace, was the only one we talked to. She said her mother was not well and in bed."

Ian scratched his head then winced, forgetting about the stitches. "Uh. Eve is not really Tobias's wife. She is mine. Grace and… uh, Chastity are ours. They are not Tobias's daughters."

That was a shock to me, and I could see that Granny and Bell were having the same feeling. I had to ask. "Uh, Ian, why were they in that other village, Sax… uh, Saxonham?"

Ian smiled at me. "That is Saxmundham. Tobias and his real wife had been taking care of Grace when she was a baby. His home at that time was much better place for her than my museum. My brother said they were glad to help."

"Real wife?" Bell questioned. "We did not see any other woman with Tobias."

"I did," I said. "I saw Tobias with a very pretty young woman in old Dunwich when storms were destroying part of the city. Ian, where is she?"

"I am sorry to say that she died many years ago. I'll tell you more about that later.

Anyway, when Eve finally returned from her abduction, I found her at the dig in Sutton Hoo."

"Abduction?" Bell and I asked.

"Yes. A few years after Eve and I arrived here, another man arrived from the past. He bound us by magic, and not the warlock kind. He kidnapped Eve. He pointed a stick at me, and I thought he was going to kill me, but Eve intervened. She silently put a protection spell on me. His attempted death spell only put me to sleep. He thought he killed me and left. When I woke, Eve was gone."

Bell and I looked at each other. Bell asked before I could. "This sounds like wizard magic. Did he have a wand? A wand that looked like a short branch with a forked end?"

"Why, yes. I do remember that. You are familiar with this type of magic?"

"Very much so," Bell replied. "We know of the last family of wizards back home. Wonderful people who we helped, and we truly love. These are the ones who escaped a plague that wiped out the entire wizarding realm—a plague brought on by an evil sorceress." I looked at Bell and we both knew what must be happening. "Uh… Ian. We did learn from them that there was a dark side in the wizard world. Sorcerers. Supposedly, they all succumbed to the plague too, but if one could have jumped time before…"

Something Ian said triggered a question from me. "Uh… Eve has abilities? Tobias said she didn't."

"Oh, very much so. I am sure she is as powerful as Yana here. I must continue. I began searching through time for Eve. Tobias tried to help but, like I said, he got ill from time traveling. I made him stay home to recuperate. I finally found Eve in Sutton Hoo… in 1939. That is why I was working at the dig. She had escaped from her captor and turned up at Edith Pretty's home, where she gave birth to Chastity. When Eve got better, she helped on the dig."

Granny had been quiet and looked deep in thought. She finally spoke. "Ian, who kidnapped Eve?"

"Lars. Lars Asulf."

Lars. I knew there was something about him I didn't like.

I wonder… "Ian, are you sure Lars actually took Eve? He made us think he snatched Granny right in front of us, but when we got back, my real Granny…" I reached over and held Granny's hand. "…was here waiting for us."

Ian nodded in understanding. "I am sure Lars took her. He can appear in solid form, but he can also appear as a specter. He is the one who had the wand you spoke of. He has the ability to travel to any time and any place he chooses. His wand is his real power. If he has a dragon ring, he might be unstoppable. By the way, Eve, Tobias, and I could also appear as specters. Hmm…" He paused and closed his eyes.

"Ian?" I asked. "Are you okay?"

"Yes, I am. You know, Lars and his men came to that Sutton Hoo area to attack us. Really to attack our cruel father. He was told about the attempted attack and along with a reluctant Tobias and several men did catch up to the last of Lars's crew as they were heading to the coast. They killed them all. Lars, with his magic stick, his wand, has been out for revenge ever since and has been ceaselessly pursuing us. All had been quiet for over ten years, so we thought Lars had finally gone to meet his ancestors. We were so wrong to be complacent."

Ian paused again. Then thought of something. "You know, the two of you, Bell, Charles, you should be able to pick and choose your time and location too. And you can also envision where to appear. As specters. It has been an awfully long time since I have taught, but I think I can show you how to do it. You can even do it with your own rings, by themselves. You do not need that third ring. That one is Eve's. She needs it back."

"We don't need this other ring?" Bell asked.

"Remember when Tobias…" Ian paused, and his voice faltered. He wiped a tear, then continued. "Sorry. I am missing my brother. Tobias mentioned how his wife… well, my wife really… was not feeling well. That was happening before you arrived and continued after you got here. She was using Tobias's ring to move around, usually as a spirit. That was her hovering over me when I was recuperating in Yana's bed. She was not going to strangle me. Also, that time when you were told Tobias and Eve left to go on holiday, well, they were both time traveling. Tobias came back exhausted while Eve continued her travels."

Now it was my turn to ask. "Why and where were they traveling? Has this got something to do with Lars?"

"Yes, it does. For centuries, we have been avoiding him. Now, we are trying to catch him. Lars was worse than our father, known as Malcolm the Cruel, who pretended to be a shaman to look important but denounced magic by murdering any who he was told were witches or warlocks. Lars was a warrior first but learned to use his wand magic to sneak in and out of time, murdering those who he believed were relations of mine and Tobias. He knew Henry Stone and I were at the Sutton Hoo dig site, and murdered Henry, probably because he had found the wand in the dig and kept it as another Sutton Hoo souvenir. Lars, I am sure, used a stolen ring to steal it back. He probably murdered Henry's grandson, Thomas, too."

Granny held up her hand for Ian to stop. "He must have snuck up and murdered my friend Garrett too."

"I am sure that is what happened. Anyway, to continue, Lars originally came to old Sutton Hoo to attack and kill Father and all the men in our village, but with his boat bogged down and so many of his men dying of fever, his goal was thwarted. He had no ability to heal the dead. Even after Eve killed Father, Lars has been trying to get to me and Tobias for centuries to get his sister back. The thing is, Eve said she is not his real sister. He called *all* his people brothers and sisters. For all this time we were trying to avoid him. Unfortunately, Tobias was thinking about me being wounded and did not look out for himself. Lars, I feel, is the one who set the explosive in Tobias's car. It might have even been an explosive from another time that he stole. And I am sure he will come after you two, especially since you met him."

I thought of something else. "Ian, do you know anything about a double-masted sailboat in Dunwich called the *Anglo Saxon*?"

"Sailboat? No. No I do not. Why do you ask?"

"It appeared in a San Francisco yacht harbor where Garrett's body was found. We also saw it in Dunwich, but only for a minute. Bell and I thought we saw a woman rowing out to the boat, but a thick fog came in. When it cleared the boat had disappeared."

"I do not know. If it was a woman, it could not be Eve. She is afraid of the ocean. It might have been Lars, but why the boat? I do not know. I have never seen it." Ian was silent for several seconds, then said, "For now, I would like to go to the museum and clean it up. I do care about my displays, even if they are reproductions. I take great pride in teaching visitors about the history of Dunwich and Sutton Hoo."

"Uh, Ian," Bell said. "Your museum has been cleaned up. So was Henry's house. We thought you and Granny did it, but it had to be someone else. Eve maybe?"

"Again, I do not know. I still want to go to my museum." Bell, Granny, and I offered to escort him there.

The door wasn't locked. Ian warned us to stand aside as he pushed it open and stepped inside. He had his hands lifted, palms facing forward, as if he was ready to protect himself from an attack. He lowered his hands.

"It is okay. You can come in now."

We walked in the front door and were shocked to see a woman sitting at Ian's desk. She looked about his age.

"Everyone. I would like you to meet my wife, Eve."

Eve was familiar. We had seen her when she arrived at Tobias's pub to cook dinner that first evening that we arrived in Saxmundham.

Eve got up from the desk and came over to give Ian a hug. As Ian introduced us, she hugged each of us in turn. "I am so happy to finally meet you in person. I am so sorry to have caused you alarm when I appeared as a spirit. That allows me to check out a location before transporting there. I was going to visit my Ian when you saw me hovering over him. I was not trying to strangle him like you thought. When you yelled, I had to abandon my transport."

Bell and I were intently listening to Eve when Granny broke in. "Eve. We know it's the griffin... your dragon ring that allows you to move about. Besides the ones you and these two have," Granny pointed at me and Bell. "...are there others who have similar rings?"

"Ian had one I made for him, but out of caution he would take it off. When he was attacked, it was stolen from his secret room along with his other artifacts. Dear Tobias..." Eve paused and sighed. "...had one too. I have been using his to get around, but it cannot be as powerful as my own."

I handed her own ring back to her. She thanked me, took Tobias's ring off and gave it to Ian.

"My dear Ian, you should destroy that ring the first chance you get." Eve suggested. "We do not want Lars to sneak in again and steal it."

Bell asked, "What about your daughters… oh, and Sven, Grace's husband?"

"Ian and I brought Chastity here to this time shortly after she was born. Then Ian returned to 1939 to continue working on the dig with his friend, Henry Stone. They both secreted artifacts, some magical, out of the digs. While Ian was there again, I stayed with Tobias to raise the girls."

"And you pretended to be Tobias's wife?" I asked.

"Tobias suggested it and kept the charade up with you that I did not know he had abilities. I did spend some time with Ian, and traveled back and forth from Saxmundham to Dunwich so I could be with my girls. When our girls became teenagers, Grace started helping Tobias and me in the pub. Unfortunately, she never learned to cook, either the natural way or the magical way."

Hmm. Tobias. "Say, Ian, Eve, the first time I started time traveling, I somehow showed up in medieval Dunwich when a huge storm started destroying the old city. I was sure I saw Tobias and a woman run by. Was Tobias married at one time?"

Ian answered. "Yes. He was married once to a lovely young mortal. Tobias told me he met her on his first time travel. They escaped their house just as it was about to fall into the sea. Sadly, she died a few years later in childbirth. The child did not live either. Tobias never got over it and started time traveling again, working in different eras until finally arriving in Saxmundham where he purchased the

Poacher's Pocket pub and stayed."

"That must be how he showed up in San Francisco in the 1920s." Granny said. "He did seem sad but got better after we dated a few times. Uh… I wonder if the gods and goddesses decided… we were meant to meet." Granny sniffed and rubbed her eyes.

"Or time travel made you meet." I suggested. Then to Eve, "Sorry to interrupt. You were saying?"

"Not a problem. We all miss Tobias. As I was saying, with the girls with him I started time traveling occasionally looking for a missing ring."

"Another ring? I assume you never found it," Granny said. "Or did you?"

"No. I am still trying to find the original ring, the one all ours are based on. I understand it came from Norway, sometime in the fifth century. I want to destroy it so Lars cannot find it and use it to increase his power even more."

Bell reached over to hold my hand then she said to Eve, "I made the two rings that Charles and I wear. How could they be related to one in the fifth century? Unless…"

"Unless?" As soon as I asked that, I sensed from Bell's mind what she meant. "Ah… yes. You think…"

"Yes. Yes. It is coming back to me. I'm remembering a short blond man came into the Mystic Eye. I'm sure he had a ring on that I kept staring at. Now that I think of it, I wonder if that could have been Lars, but I really can't remember. I believe now I was forced to forget. I also remember I couldn't see anything in his eyes. I was barely sixteen but still sensed he had abilities. However, he didn't talk and only looked around. There was shining amber that caught my eye, and I felt compelled to make the rings. It had to be a spell that made me start making the two rings we now wear. Eve, could that guy's ring have been the original?"

"Maybe. The same thing happened to me when I was sixteen. That's when I also made two rings. However, it could not have been... uh, Lars back then. I did not know of him yet. Bell, can you remember the date you were visited?"

"It was at least a year before I met Charles. Ah, yes, I think I remember. The day was so foggy we couldn't see across the street. Yana?"

"Your mother and I were nervous about that fog and that short man. He and the fog appeared out of nowhere. And the fog seemed to be only along Broadway and down to the bay. Charles, one of my notebooks would have the date. I remember writing about the unusually thick fog that day. I seem to recall writing something about the blond man too. He was dressed kind of odd. We'll have to look through my library for that notebook."

"Granny, what if Bell and I used our rings to head back to San Francisco and find the date in that notebook of yours? Then we can zip back here and let Eve know what day and time it was so she can travel there."

"Why don't we all go there?" Bell suggested.

"We could go to San Francisco to get the notebook, but we won't be able to go back in time to the Mystic Eye. Only Eve could go there. Bell, you and I should not be in two places at once. No telling what kind of problem could occur. Hmm. Charles, since you hadn't met Bell yet maybe you could go with Eve. Eve, would that be okay?"

"Yes. I have grown older living so long in this time and could use your help. Especially since Charles has so many abilities. If we do run into that blond man and he happens to be Lars, we should be able to keep him from casting spells on us. You said you are familiar with wizards. I am not. Yes, I could use your help."

"Okay," I said. "For now, Bell and I will transport ourselves home. We should also check in with Patrick and bring him up to speed."

"Who is this Patrick?" Eve asked. "Is he trustworthy? Is he one of us?"

"He is. Patrick is a retired police homicide detective who recently found out about his warlock abilities. Very few abilities so far. Yana, here, has been training him to increase them. He is a very good friend. Now, Bell, let's think about going home. Uh… We only have our own rings though."

Ian said, "Remember, I told you that you do not need Eve's ring. You can use your own to travel wherever or whenever you choose. You have to believe in it."

We held hands, did the ring thing again and with our own rings. We really concentrated on our destination. And it worked.

We appeared in the center of Granny's living room. I moved before my eyes totally cleared up from our ring's bright flash and bumped my shin on her coffee table.

"Ow! Crud! That hurt! That's going to leave a bruise."

I took a couple of steps back from the coffee table and nearly tripped over an ottoman. Bell reprimanded me.

"Stop moving, lover, until our eyes clear up."

Finally, a minute later, our eyes did clear up.

"Bell, I need a little water. How about you?"

She did. We went into Granny's kitchen, filled two glasses, and quickly downed them.

"Ah. That's better. Okay, let's head upstairs."

Granny's office and library faced the back of the house.

We turned around the stairwell railing and walked into the room.

"Now, Bell, Granny said her notebooks were hidden in a bag in that closet." I pointed to it. The door was in the corner next to one of the floor-to-ceiling bookcases we got for Granny.

I opened the door and pulled out a carpetbag, very similar to the bottomless one she always carried with her with all her traveling clothes and other items. I pulled it out and set it on Granny's new desk next to her old Underwood typewriter. I opened the bag.

"Well. Granny did say it would look empty."

I closed it and recited a spell Granny told me to say. I opened it again, and it was full of notebooks.

"Okay, Bell. Let's find the ones from when you were sixteen. What year was that? Ah. 1961. That's a year before my parents were...."

"Don't think about that, lover. Let's look through these notebooks. Yana has them stacked in order. And...."

"And here's the first one from 1961. Here's three more from that same year. Granny was writing quite a bit back then."

We sat down cross legged on the oriental carpet. Bell grabbed one notebook, I took another, and we started reading the journal entries. Each notebook covered three months out of the year.

Bell barely looked at the notebook she had and set it down. "I'm not yet sixteen in this one. My birthday is in April. The fog and that guy must be in one of the other three notebooks."

"And here's an entry Granny wrote mentioning your birthday. Some ceremony she and your mother gave you."

"Of course," Bell said softly. "My sixteenth birthday and witchy coming of age party at our Telegraph Hill home." She sighed. "Garrett was there."

"That's what Granny wrote here. Uh… also friends from school? Non-ability kids?"

"Yeah. Mom wanted some of my Galileo High School friends to come to my party. Make it seem normal. Mom and Yana, and even Garrett made sure my friends wouldn't remember the witchy part when they left."

"There's mentions of some customers, both normal and with abilities, but no mention of a strange fog. Only… here she wrote about a foggy day, but it sounds like any normal San Francisco day."

Bell and I picked up the other two notebooks from 1961 and started scanning the pages.

"Bell. Here's one. Granny writes 'Two hours have gone by and no customers yet. Perhaps the thick fog is the problem. Constance went to pick up Bell from school. She plans to work on costumes upstairs.' That's all for that entry. June 10."

"Charles, here's another reference to fog. This is dated August 10. 'Unusually foggy outside for a warm August. It appears to be only in front of the Mystic Eye and down past the Embarcadero freeway. Sunny the other direction up Broadway. Like last time it was foggy, no customers yet. Bell is helping me unload a shipment. Two hours after opening a customer finally came in. A single stranger with abilities I could feel but couldn't tell what they were. Handsome short blue-eyed blond man. He was oddly dressed in leather and with a hood made of fur over his head. Some hippie? No purchases. Bell and I did notice his lovely ring. She wants to make one like it.' Jeez, Charles, I remember feeling compelled to make not just one, but two for some reason. For you? I didn't know you yet. You know I never did any jewelry making before, but I somehow knew exactly what to do."

"Yeah. You must have been spellbound. Is there anything else Granny wrote about that?"

"She mentions that the fog lifted shortly after the blond man left. Also, she says that two small pieces of amber were left on the counter. She figures that man left them, but she didn't see him drop them off."

"Okay. When we return to Dunwich, we'll tell Eve the date and time. I remember Granny or your mother opened the shop at 11 am. Eve and I could be there then."

"Uh… Charles. Granny wrote that there were no customers for a couple of hours. If you and Eve show up, will that change history somehow? Will Granny's notebook change?"

"That's right. My parents were still alive. Granny didn't take me in for another year. I would be seen as a customer, but Granny would know who I am. We need to talk to Eve about that. We might have to figure out another plan. Now. Let's go call Patrick."

Chapter 17

Patrick wasn't home. I dialed the police department and got Castillo. He said he and Patrick had been at a morning briefing and then went out to check the yacht harbor again. Patrick just left and should be home soon. I congratulated Castillo on his promotion to Captain. He thanked me, and we hung up.

"Well. Patrick should be home shortly. I'm curious about why they went back to the yacht harbor. I mean, there's no ship at the dock anymore where Garrett was found."

"Unless the ship returned."

"We can't leave to go check it out. Patrick would tell us if it's there again. I'll call again in ten minutes. For now, let's see what Granny has in her refrigerator. I'm feeling a little uh… peckish."

We nibbled on a couple of pieces of cheddar, and an apple Bell sliced up. When we were done, I called Patrick again. He was home.

"Hey, Patrick. Charles here. Just wanted to check in to see how you're doing. Any news?"

"You're not going to believe this, but that sailboat, the Anglo Saxon was back. Castillo and I went to the dock but couldn't get through the gate. I mumbled an incantation while Castillo was walking away and tried to unlock it, but I still can't do that like Bell or Yana can. I need more lessons. So, we went to the yacht harbor office to see about getting a key for the dock, and the woman there insisted there was no two-masted boat there. When we pointed out the window, a thick fog had come in so we couldn't see the boat. The woman did give Castillo the key to the dock, but when we went back, the boat was gone again. Yeah, completely gone, just disappeared. Castillo figured the boat was on the bay in the fog. I wasn't going to tell him otherwise. Say, are you guys back?"

"Again, only temporary. And this is something you're not going to believe. The rings Bell and I wear allow us to not only transport ourselves to and from England, but we can also time travel. I know that sounds impossible, but..."

"Uh, yeah. That is hard for me to fathom. Oh. What were you about to say?"

"You know, I just thought of something. I think Bell thought of it too. She's nodding her head yes. Our time trips have two things in common. When the other rings were made, and when one was found and stolen from the dig by Henry Stone... yes, Patrick, Garrett Stone's brother. Both Henry and Ian Malcolm, who we met here, were hired diggers on the Sutton Hoo ship burial archeological site."

"So, you've been where? When?"

"I've been to the dig site three times from 1939 to 1941. That 1941 trip was short because the Second World War was happening. I think we were there quite by accident. I think. Anyway, Bell and I also went back to the 7th century in the same area the buried ship was found. What we found there I'll tell you after we really come home."

"So. Have you found out anything about those strange murders? I can't see or find anything from this end. Castillo is really frustrated that he can't find any clues."

"We think it's a guy named Lars Asulf who may be the perp. I say we think because we're not totally sure yet. We do think he's trying to steal back the rings and maybe other artifacts to increase his power. Yeah, Patrick, this guy is from the past. Another time traveler. And I think he is a wizard… or probably a sorcerer. He has a wand. That's what gives him the ability to send others across time and space. That might be what weakened Thomas, but, again, we're not sure. Garrett, we are sure, died in England. I think he was hit on the head with the same weapon that almost killed Ian. Maybe that sailboat we've seen in the harbor is what he was brought back in. Well, that's just conjecture right now."

"Jeez, Charles. The more you and Bell do, the more I know I'll never learn it all. At my age? No. I'll just have to be satisfied with the little I can pick up from Yana's lessons. Oh. Is Yana there too?"

"No. She's still in Dunwich with Ian. Ha. Another story I'll have to tell you later. Right now, Bell and I must get back to England. Our original plan to confront this Lars guy fell through. We need to make new plans."

"Be really careful you two. And please get back safely."

After I hung up, Bell and I went back upstairs and put Granny's notebooks away, then we went downstairs to the same spot we arrived at and prepared to use the rings to transport us back to Dunwich.

"Okay, Bell, ready? Scotty, beam us up."

As we arrived back in Dunwich, I was chuckling about my

Star Trek reference. Bell never watched the show and looked at me askance. One of these days I'll have to see if any Star Trek reruns are on TV so Bell can understand some of the iconic phrases from that show.

Well, anyway, it did seem that Bell and I are getting used to the rings moving us around the world. We were still a little thirsty, but it did seem we were doing better. We were now back in Ian's museum.

However, we were alone. Ian, Eve, and Granny were not around.

"Bell, let's get a little drink from the water cooler here and then go find the others."

"If she's close, we should be able to contact her telepathically."

I spoke first trying to get a response, then Bell did the same. No luck.

"Your Granny might be at the Stone house scrying and not to be disturbed."

"I don't know why she's scrying there now, but, anyway, let's go next door and see if Ian and Eve are there, then try to contact Granny again."

The Ship Inn pub was busy. Another tour bus had pulled up and the place was full. No Ian or Eve. We went upstairs. Granny's room was not locked, but peeking in, we could see her satchel was still on the floor by her bed.

"If Granny was somewhere scrying, she would have her satchel with her."

"Charles, I have an odd feeling. Do you feel it? The cold?"

"Crud! That feels like the same cold we experienced at that grave. Could it be Lars again? Was he here and really took Granny?"

"Before we attempt to use our rings again, we should get out to Henry Stone's house and check there first. Just in case."

Bell and I ran all the way to the house. The door was still locked with the spell Bell put on it.

"Granny's not here!" Bell could see I was getting upset. She reached down and drew my hand up to my medicine bag. It was more of Bell touching me than my medicine bag that eased my mind.

Then she put her hand on the door and closed her eyes.

"Charles. There is someone in there. I'm going to unlock the door."

My head started to ache again. The pain was increasing, and I began to black out. Before Bell had a chance to unlock the door, she heard me groan and turned in time to catch me as I fell.

I didn't close my eyes to darkness. Behind my eyelids I could see a bright light, similar to the flash we see when our rings sent us to other times and places. In that light I saw, or imagined I saw, a frightened young woman in 7th century Sutton Hoo motioning to me. She looked familiar.

Chastity?

Chapter 18

As quickly as the headache came on, it dissipated. I opened my eyes to see Bell's worried expression as she held my head in her hands and stroked my face.

"Oh, lover, you're back. I was so worried. Are you okay?"

"Yeah. Yeah. I think so. That migraine was really bad."

We kept talking as we walked back to the inn. Bell led me into our room. I plopped down on the chair. Bell sat on the edge of the bed facing me. "You came to, but you didn't use your medicine bag."

"No. It went away on its own. Bell, love, I have to tell you what I saw. It was like scrying, but I think the vision was forced on me. I saw Chastity in, I think, the 7th century. She is one of Ian's and Eve's daughters. And she looked scared of something."

"Chastity? I don't know who that is."

"Oh yeah. I have to tell you about her."

I related to Bell how Chastity exposed herself and tried to seduce me, and how angry she got when her attempts failed.

"Do you think this Chastity is causing your headaches? She sounds like she might be a dark witch."

"Maybe, but I don't think so. Her older sister is married to a regular human and seems nice. No, I don't think Chastity is causing my migraines. Besides, I was getting these headaches before we came to Dunwich. I really think something else is causing them."

"I still don't understand why only you are getting headaches. If it was some warlock or witch spell, all of us should be feeling it. Why just you?"

Yeah. Why just me? And why did I have that vision of Chastity when I was out this time? And why the attack that almost killed Ian and left me in a coffin? Who did that? Lars? And what about that two-masted sailboat that keeps appearing and disappearing? Who is piloting that? And, more importantly, where's Granny… and Ian and Eve?

"Lover, where did you go? I can't even hear your thoughts."

"Sorry, Bell. I was just trying to work things out in my mind. I have a lot of questions and no answers yet. Grandfather's spirit guide has helped me before, and somehow usually knows what is happening. You know, I wish you could see and hear him like I do."

Bell was quiet, then blurted out, "Peter Red Feather! Charles! Your grandfather! You know that's the one thing different about you than the rest of us. It's your Ohlone side. Your shamanism. Could that be why only you get migraines?"

"But why? Shamanism never affected me like this before. I can't see that Grandfather is causing this. Maybe…" I drifted off into thought again.

Bell put her hand on my arm. "Maybe?"

"Sorry. Yeah, maybe someone or something is affecting my shaman side. Who else is a shaman who we've been around or that we know?"

"The only one I can think of was that one the wizard Dean Prentiss introduced us to in that Miwok village he called us to last year."

"Yeah. Not him. I had no problem there. There is Arwald, Malcolm the Cruel, who claimed he was one, but Ian and Tobias both said that was not true. Who else?"

"What about Lars? Could he be a Nordic shaman? I mean, he's lied to us about Ian and about kidnapping Granny. He has powers of some kind. Like you have both warlock and shaman powers, could he be like you? Both warlock and shaman? Or is he wizard… or sorcerer and shaman?"

"But, again, we had no idea that Lars existed, and I was getting headaches before we came to England."

"Yeah. But what if after we saw Lars when we thought he took Granny, he traveled back to a time we were home. A time before we came to England."

"That sounds impossible, but we used to think time traveling was impossible. So… crud. I don't know.

We were both quiet in thought. I was trying to remember the first time I got a migraine.

Bell was thinking the same thing. "When did your…"

"Headaches start? Yeah. When?"

"I think it was right after you and me and Yana went to get Garrett's notebook from Thomas's apartment."

"Could that person Mac saw leave be the one causing my migraines? Lars maybe?" I reached over and held Bell's hand. "But… Bell, love, we must find Granny."

We checked the museum one more time. Still, no one there, and no evidence of anyone being there recently. A half hour later, we arrived at Henry's old house. Someone had been there since we were earlier. The door was now ajar.

Before entering, Bell did a mental scan. "There's no one inside this time."

"Maybe they were here earlier."

We entered and were met by an apparition. A woman's apparition who seemed to be looking around the room. She seemed startled to see us and quickly disappeared.

"Bell, you said there was no one inside."

"No solid person. I couldn't see that ghostly being. Who was that?"

"That was Chastity. She must have taken Tobias's ring before Ian could destroy it. Eve said she could scan a destination before appearing. That must be what Chastity was doing."

"Do you think she's the one who hit you and Ian?"

"I really can't see her doing that. Ian is her father. Bell, I'm really worried about Granny. I can't even locate her with telepathy."

"I hate to say this, but she might be traveling with Ian and Eve... either somewhere or some time. I think we should go to Saxmundham and confront this Chastity. We could either take the bus, or..."

"Let's go."

We held hands and put our rings together. I envisioned the room I stayed in at Tobias's pub. Since we were going a short distance, when our rings glowed, it was not as bright as before.

We reappeared in the room I had stayed in. Fortunately, it was vacant. I hadn't thought about what would have happened if someone was staying there. Now I see why Eve always checked beforehand as a specter. I'd have to try that next time.

"Whew. No one here. Bell, can you envision anyone in the hall outside?"

"No. We should go downstairs. Sounds like a lot of people are down there."

"Yeah. But first, let's see if Chastity is up here."

Two doors down was Chastity's room. Bell scanned inside. "No. She's not in there. Well, unless she's still ghostly."

"I doubt if she would do that in her own room. Let's head downstairs."

As we descended the stairs, we could see the place was full. American tourists. A big bus sat by the curb in front. Obviously, Grace was serving. Each table had a bowl of sliced bread, a block of cheese, and a pitcher of beer. Several of the tourists were attempting to play darts, and a couple others were pulling the handles on the two slot machines. They were noisy and didn't even notice us coming down the stairs.

Sven did.

He came out from behind the bar and stood in front of us with his muscular arms crossed. "What the hell do you think you're doing? Why were you upstairs? You better have a good reason before I throw you out."

"He started to take hold of Bell's arm to lead her out but couldn't touch her. She had her arms crossed too. It was as if Sven's hand hit a brick wall. It hurt and he yelped. He tried to do the same to me. I copied Bell and crossed my arms. Again, it hurt him, and he yelped again.

His eyes grew wide with fright and backed away just as Grace came over to see why her husband was having trouble with us. When she saw who we were, she smiled and put her hand on Sven's shoulder. That relaxed him, and he went back behind the bar, again smiling and serving his customers.

"Ah. Good to see you again mister Blue. And you must be Miss Beltane."

"Please call me Bell."

"And please call me Charles. Sorry we upset your husband."

"Sven tries to be so protective of this establishment. Especially since we lost Tobias. This place really belongs to mom and dad now. But with them running off on their quests, Sven and I came in to help."

"What about your sister?" Bell asked. "We just saw her in Dunwich."

"Dunwich? That couldn't have been her. This morning after breakfast, she went back upstairs, and I haven't seen her come back down."

"Well, she's not in her room now," I said. "By the way. It wasn't her real self we saw in Dunwich. It was her ghostly image, and she was looking around in the Henry Stone house."

"What? How? She couldn't. She wouldn't…"

"Does she have a griffin ring?" Bell asked. "Like these?" Both of us held our hands out showing Grace our rings.

"I don't think so. But Tobias did… Oh. Sven's calling me over. I need to serve some more ale to these American tourists. They can really drink a lot. We can talk more when this crowd clears out."

After she left, I turned to Bell. "Chastity must have stolen Tobias's ring and is just learning to use it. She must have noticed mine and recognized it as like Tobias's. "

"Maybe that happened. If Chastity did steal it, and you told me about her trying to seduce you, that makes her seem like she might really be a problem child."

"But how did she find out how to use the ring?" I said, tapping my own ring for emphasis. "Eve said she can become ghostly when preparing to travel. Could Chastity have witnessed Eve doing that and is now doing the same?"

"Or did she discover it on her own? Kind of like we did."

I couldn't counter that idea. But another thought came into my mind. "That last big headache caused me to see Chastity in old Sutton Hoo. She seemed scared when I envisioned her. Maybe she ran into Lars."

"Everything we're coming up with is just speculation. You know, Charles, we can't get distracted right now. We have to find Yana."

Chapter 19

Activity in the pub was increasing. Another van full of people showed up. This time all English, and all carrying cameras and binoculars. Obviously, a group of birdwatchers. A very thirsty group of birdwatchers. We wouldn't be able to talk to Grace for quite a while.

As she was serving several more pints to the standing only crowd, I came up to her and told her we had to go, but we'd try to get back later.

Instead of sneaking back upstairs to travel back to Dunwich, we went outside behind the pub. We hid beside a dumpster and looked back and forth to make sure no one was around. We disappeared and reappeared back in our room in Dunwich.

"Bell, I'm getting an odd feeling we should head back to Henry's house again. Before we go, let's go see if Granny left any clue to where she went."

Granny's door was now locked, but Bell mumbled a couple of words and quickly opened it. Inside, I noticed right away that Granny must have slept here last night. Her bed was roughly made, as was her habit. Her satchel was on the floor. The satchel she always took with her. That was odd. Unless… I opened it thinking I would find only one or two scrying pieces.

"Bell. Look here. It seems Granny has been busy. There are at least six things wrapped up in cheesecloth."

"Really? When and where did she get all these? Uh, Charles, do you think you could scry with them?"

"I don't know. I'll carefully open these one at a time without touching anything to see what's in here. I don't want to mess up Granny's scrying pieces."

"Yes. Be careful. Maybe these will clue us in to where Yana has been… and maybe still is."

I pulled the first of the wrapped-up items out of the bag and unfolded it.

"It's a piece of colored glass. Old colored glass. Hmm. I wonder if it came from Stone's house?"

Bell gave an I-don't-know shrug.

I unwrapped the second piece.

"This is weird. It looks like part of a bracelet. Look here. That's pretty sophisticated carving on it. I think I saw this at the Sutton Hoo dig when I first went there in 1939. But I think Basil Brown had it."

"That's strange. Are you getting any scrying feelings?"

"Nothing. Let me try the next one."

As I unwrapped the third one, I felt another headache coming on.

"Bell! Bell! Something's happening." I told her as I squeezed my eyes closed tightly.

"What? What is that thing?"

I held in my hand a finger bone. Not Thomas's either. A finger bone with a ring still on it. A dragon ring. It started to glow.

"Charles! Drop that! Grab your medicine bag! Quick!"

Before I could do so, I saw a bright light behind my eyelids again. This time I saw teenage Ian in ancient Sutton Hoo. He was running away from a village with Eve. A very young Eve.

I felt my hand on my medicine bag. Bell must have placed it there. As quickly as the headache came on, it disappeared. Or so I thought.

When I came to, I was lying down on the floor next to Granny's satchel. Bell was rubbing my forehead with a cold washcloth. She had tears in her eyes.

"Oh, Bell. That feels good. How long was I out this time?"

"Twenty minutes. Please, please stop scaring me like that. I thought you were gone for good. You didn't seem to be breathing."

"Really? I'm so sorry to scare you, Bell. For some reason, I felt I was only out a few seconds. You know this hurts a lot when it happens. This is not fun."

"Maybe you should put these pieces back in Yana's bag."

"We haven't seen them all yet. I'm hoping at least one of these will give us a clue as to where Granny is."

I pulled the fourth piece out of Granny's satchel and unwrapped it.

"It's the other half of that bracelet. How did Granny get these? I know these were with Basil Brown. I saw the second piece brought to him."

"So has Yana traveled back in time?"

"Wait a minute. Bell, these are not Granny's. Look at this cheesecloth. This one isn't coated with her neutralizing agent."

I pulled all the wrapped pieces out of Granny's satchel and laid them side by side. Only the first one I opened, the piece of glass, had the real neutralized cheesecloth. The five others were wrapped in plain cheesecloth.

"Bell. Someone other than us has been in Granny's bag. I am getting a scrying feeling now. And it's not from the items. It's from the cheesecloth. These things were stolen. Someone is maybe trying to change history."

"Jeez! Not good! Can you see who it is?"

"No. I've been trying, but I'm blocked. I can only see what I told you."

"Charles, maybe someone is trying to change history in 1939, or maybe even earlier, say back in the 7th century. Or…"

"Or? Oh. You think maybe someone is just trying to steal as many Sutton Hoo pieces as they can?"

"Well remember, Henry Stone was selling off his collection to pay for his gambling debts. Ian kept his, and several were stolen when Ian was attacked. Now we're seeing pieces in this satchel we know were with Basil Brown. Yes. It does look like someone is stealing the artifacts from different times."

"What else is in the other two wrappings?"

I opened both and laid them out on the floor.

"These are…"

"Both from the British Museum." This was said by someone who appeared out of nowhere and stood behind us. When we turned around, we were shocked at who we saw.

"Tobias?"

"The one and only."

"I saw your car go up in flames with you inside. How did… ah. You do have a ring. Who was in your car?"

"Oh, just some poor peasant I transferred there from

my… uh, father's dungeon."

"You brought someone here from the 7ᵗʰ century?" Bell asked.

"Why not. My bro… father was going to hang him anyway. He was accused of being a witch. Well, a warlock, really. Father doesn't know the difference."

Tobias was definitely not the friendly innkeeper we first met. His face was contorted with anger, and he was trying to swing a 7ᵗʰ century war ax, obviously the one he hit me and Ian with. Granny's room was small with a low ceiling. It would be hard for him to swing it hard at us. We were keeping the bed between us and him. I got the feeling he was getting ready to jump at Bell and me and dispatch us. I wanted to keep him talking. "Why did you fake your death?"

"You don't need to know that."

"Did you attack your brother? And me?"

"Ian should have died!" Tobias yelled. "You showed up and did some weird shaman witch thing and kept him alive! I hate you for that." He was pointing at us with the ax. He kept ranting. "Ian took away… the only woman I loved! I deserved her! I wanted her! When… father took me on one of his raids, Ian stayed home and then disappeared with Eve! I hated him."

Something he said sounded off to me. I had to keep him going. "Were you responsible for Henry Stone's death? And his nephew's? And Garrett's?"

He smiled. Not a nice smile at all. "Oh yeah. Henry had all those nice artifacts, but the bastard ended up selling most of them. Henry was in bed recuperating from a beating some guys gave him and wouldn't tell me where he sold the pieces. I pulled him up and took him back to Sutton Hoo in

1939 to steal his pieces there. No luck. Too many people around. When he saw himself in the dig, he collapsed, and when I brought him back to Dunwich to force him once more to tell me where his artifacts were sold, he was dead. I couldn't leave him in his house where someone might notice him shriveling up, so I buried him."

"Did you send for Henry's nephew the news of his uncle's death?"

"I did not understand why he showed up. But I'm glad he did. He had on one of the dragon rings. Henry must have given it to him."

"I doubt that. Henry had a safe deposit box in Ipswich that had a few Sutton Hoo pieces in it. The ring was there. But why cut his finger off?"

"The ring would not pull off. I traveled back to my cas... my home in the 7th century with the unconscious jerk and cut his finger off then sent him back to his home, wherever that was."

"San Francisco. The same city you sent Garrett back to."

"The kid, yes! That other guy, no. I just tossed him into the ocean."

"Why did you come back and open the graves and steal the bodies?"

"What the gods are you talking about? I only buried Henry. I did not remove him. Or any other body. I know of no other body."

"It was an ancient body that was partially under Henry's. It was taken along with Henry's body."

"I did not remove any bodies. His body is gone?"

"Yep. And all the artifacts from Ian's museum. Did you take those too?"

"When I got there all the cabinets were open and empty.

Ian must have hidden them elsewhere. I was so angry I lashed out and hit him. God. I was sure he was dead. If I'd known he was still alive, I would have finished him off. But I heard someone coming, so I disappeared."

"But why did you bury me in that coffin?"

"I still do not know how you got out of that. I put a curse on the box and was about to push it over the cliff when I heard someone else talking close by. I was interrupted again. I had to disappear quickly."

Bell had been standing next to me and being very calm and quiet. She had her arms crossed. She had heard something in her head. It was not telepathy. She looked at me and smiled. I looked at her with a questioning squint.

Tobias started to come around the bed toward us, his war ax ready to swing.

Bell yelled. "Now!"

"What?" Tobias stopped, nearly running into Eve, Grace, and Granny who appeared right in front of us, between us and Tobias, who jumped back bumping into the dresser, his eyes wide in fright.

Eve calmly walked up to Tobias and slapped him hard, nearly toppling him over. He dropped his war ax, and Eve quickly picked it up and threatened him with it. "You have a lot of nerve pretending to be a good brother." She kept walking toward him with the ax head pointing at his face. He kept trying to back away then turned to run out the door. I could see his ring getting bright.

Eve grabbed his arm before he could escape and the two of them disappeared together.

"Mom!" Grace yelled, running up to where they disappeared.

Granny touched my arm. "Help me, dear Charles."

She sat on the bed, about to collapse. I grabbed my medicine bag. Time stood still for both me and Granny. Grandfather, Peter Red Feather, appeared sitting next to Granny and put his hand on her shoulder.

"My dear Yana. Open your eyes. You are okay. It is not your time to join me."

Granny opened her eyes and tears began dripping down her cheeks. "My wonderful Peter. Oh, how I miss you."

"And I miss you, dear Yana. But through our young shaman here, I will always be around. Yana, you are healed." Grandfather recited the same healing spell that I use. Granny sighed. Grandfather left, and time returned.

"Mom! Grace yelled, running up to where they disappeared. I thought I saw that already.

Granny was fine. She got up and walked over to Grace. "Don't worry Grace. Your mother knows what to do. I'm sure she'll be back soon, and with your sister, Chastity, in tow.

"So, Chastity has been back in the 7th century," I said. "Granny, I thought I dreamt that. I saw her as a very scared girl who looked as if she was being chased."

"Dear Charles, you have a very odd scrying ability. I have never, in my long life, ever seen such an ability. Oh. Are you getting any more headaches?"

"Had one a while ago, but that's when I envisioned Chastity. I really hope they are over. Uh… say, Granny, what about that two-masted boat we keep seeing around. Grace? Do you know anything about that?"

"No. I don't. Is it from the past?"

"No. It's a typical modern-style sailboat. It might be older, but it is from the twentieth century."

"Well, maybe Mom knows."

"Knows what?" Eve was back and with a tight grip on Chastity's arm.

Chastity looked very sheepish, her head down. She was also crying.

Chapter 20

Grace and her mother hugged. Grace started to hug her sister, but Chastity stepped back and looked at her in anger. She started screaming at her.

"Damn you! You're a perfect daughter and goddam perfect wife! I've always wanted what you have! I tried! Oh, how I tried! I could never compete with you my whole life!" Tears were streaming down her cheeks.

Grace was tearing up too. "Compete? I'm hurt you think that way about me. Chastity, we are sisters. I love you. Neither of us is better than the other. Plus, you are so much prettier than me. You do not have to envy me."

Chastity wiped away her tears and talked haltingly through sniffling. "But… but you have… you have such a nice… nice handsome man. I… was going to run away with my own man who… who really wanted me, but Mother… she came and took me… me from him and left him…lying helpless on the ground."

Eve let go of Chastity's arm. It was then I noticed something was in Eve's other closed hand. But before I could ask, Eve turned face to face with Chastity.

"I had to cast a spell on him to show him he cannot jump every young girl he comes across. And Lars cannot and would not be husband for you back in the 7th century. If you…" Eve paused, then continued. "If you coupled with him, you would change history as we know it. I should have told you this years ago. Lars is your father."

"Mother, he is not! He seemed so interested in me… for myself!"

"Of course, he would say that. He only wanted his manhood to use you, like so many of the warriors from that era who used the many women they captured and made slaves of… like me… when I was too weak to fight back. Not like now. No, he cannot couple with you." Eve paused again, looked thoughtful, then said, "Look, Chastity, Lars is your real father. And no, Grace, do not worry, your father really is Ian. I am married to him. You two were born a year apart. Chastity, it would be incest if Lars had you. That is why you cannot be with him."

Holy cow! I thought. Bell and Granny were thinking the same thing. Granny said to us telepathically, "*I didn't see that coming.*"

Eve heard Granny's thoughts and smiled at her. "Now. I heard something about a boat. Describe it please."

Bell and I described the boat and all the events that seemed to happen around it, especially showing up in San Francisco with the body of Garrett in tow.

"I am so sorry about your friend. I am also sorry I cannot help you. I know nothing about that boat. Personally, I do not feel safe on the ocean. It does frighten me."

"Ian mentioned that," I noted. "By the way. What did you do with Tobias? Did you kill him?"

"No, I did not. But he will not be able to travel through time or place ever again. See?" Eve opened her hand. It was a freshly severed finger with a dragon ring on it. It almost turned my stomach, but then I thought of how Tobias deceived us all and caused all the deaths and had done the same with Thomas's finger. Odd. The finger looked too small to be from Tobias's large hands.

"So, Eve, what will you do with that ring?" I asked.

"Watch." Eve had Tobias's war ax strapped to her back side. I hadn't noticed that at first because her back was turned away from us. She pulled it out, set the finger and ring on the floor, swung the ax, and completely severed the ring and half the remaining finger… and left a big dent in the floor. The ring, now broken, turned to dust, as did the remaining finger. "Now, Tobias and that ring will never cause trouble again. He is now stuck in the 7th century."

"But what if he digs up the buried ship in Sutton Hoo?" I asked.

"Impossible. I put a protection spell on the burial mound. It will not be found until 1939, as we well know it was."

"That's a relief." I let out a breath I'd been holding. "Now, Eve, any idea why someone is stealing all the Sutton Hoo artifacts?"

"That I do not know. Whoever took them has not shown themselves yet. It might have been Lars, but I really do not think so."

Bell suggested, "Maybe it is whoever is piloting that two-masted sailboat that keeps showing up here and in San Francisco."

"If that could be true, I wonder about their motive. Why steal artifacts? And why was Garrett found by it? Will we ever find out?"

"I would ask the same questions." Granny said. "You said that boat disappeared almost immediately after you saw it in Dunwich?"

"We didn't see it disappear, Granny. Bell and I saw someone rowing an inflatable boat out to it, then we got distracted. When we turned back, there was a bank of real thick fog. When it dissipated, the boat was gone."

"Patrick saw the same thing happen in San Francisco. There was thick fog, then the boat disappeared. Uh… Granny, remember the thick fog you said happened that time in the Mystic Eye? Are you sure it was a man who came in with the ring that Bell copied?"

"That was so long ago. The person was dressed like a man. But didn't talk. I was not able to hear any telepathic thoughts either. Whoever it was did have some kind of ability. But that person was only there for a few minutes at most with a hood up. Like I wrote, the fog dissipated as soon as the person left. Bell, can you remember anything different?"

"No, Yana. I only remember getting the urge to make these rings. I'm sure I was spellbound. After all, I was only sixteen and my abilities were not strong yet."

"Well, children, if a very thick fog appears again, we will be ready for whoever or whatever shows up. Bell, I know you can close your eyes and see through doors and walls and other things to know if someone is on the other side. You might be able to do that through the fog. Maybe Charles could do that too. I know I do not have that ability. Eve? Do you or your daughters have the ability?"

"Sorry, Yana, no. That has never been… oh." Eve had raised her hand as emphasis and noticed what was on her finger. "Wait. My ring. Charles. Bell. Your rings too. Maybe that adds to your abilities and allows you see what is on the other side of doors and walls. I can travel as a spirit to check out a place before I appear solid there. Maybe I, too, could help if that thick fog shows up again. Yes?"

"We may all need help when, and if, that time comes," Granny commented. "The thing is, we don't know what to expect or from what time and place it is coming from. Hopefully, we won't have to do battle."

"I don't think we will," I said. "Whoever is in the boat has not attacked us. It was always Tobias. The one thing that does bother me is how Garrett turned up with that boat?"

Chastity spoke up. "My… father, Lars, has some kind of power. He said he's something called a shaman. Mother? Do you know what he means?"

"You should ask Mister Blue. Charles, here."

I nodded. "I am also a shaman. See this on my neck? This is called a medicine bag. American Indians also have shamans. I am descended from an American West tribe called the Ohlone. This medicine bag allows me many ways to help people… and myself if I come to harm. I am also descended from my grandmother's Roma background, which is my warlock side. Yes, I am a warlock and a shaman. And, I believe your father, Lars, has some kind of wizard, or sorcerer, background, since he uses a branch-like wand and can do magic spells. Bell and I are very familiar with wizards. He may be a Scandinavian, or some Nordic tribal shaman too."

Chastity looked confused. I tried again. "Look. Your father is two things. A wizard and a shaman. Depending on his own upbringing, one could be stronger than the other. How did he seem to you when you were with him?"

"He was… I don't know. He was waving his stick around,

and I felt like I needed to go with him. I was scared and started to run but stopped. I would have gone with him if mother hadn't showed up."

"And he would have forced you to couple with him," Eve angrily said. "He sees a pretty girl, and all he can think of is 'oh… I want to be inside her.'" Eve said that with a deep voice like a man. "Chastity, my dear, you are pretty and can pick and choose whoever you want to be with… or marry. But please be aware, some… but not all… men would use you one time and then throw you away. That is the way of the old warriors." Eve pointed at us. Why… look at these two. Charles and Bell." *Huh?* Bell and I thought. "These two are really in love. This can happen to you too, Chastity. Be patient, my young witch. It will happen one day."

Bell and I did have our arms around each other while listening to Eve. I asked, "Eve, your daughters have abilities through you, and through their fathers. I've never seen them use any. Why?"

"Grace is a quite powerful witch, having a warlock father and me."

Chastity was again looking at Grace with anger. She started to say something, but Eve raised a finger and shushed her.

"Thank you. Now. Chastity has my witch side and Lars's wizard and shaman side. If she would not try to seduce every man she sees, and practiced her abilities…"

"Mother! Not every man… "

"Shush! Chastity, dear, you have so much power, but you have never learned to use it properly. When you are older… and, I hope, wiser, you should be able to be very helpful to all our kind… and also to… normal people."

"Mother, I did seem to understand one thing I heard Lars

say to me in his language. I fell when running from him and cut my hand. I think he used a healing spell. My hand healed."

Chastity closed her eyes and said a couple of words in the old Norse language. As soon as she said that my head felt like it was going to split open. Another major migraine. Bell couldn't hold me up. I fell to the floor and blacked out.

"Chastity!" Eve yelled. "What did you do?"

Chastity sat down hard on the floor next to me, her hand to her mouth and fear in her eyes. "I don't know. I don't know. It is supposed to be a healing spell."

"No one here needed healing. This man is also a shaman. Your spell worked the opposite on him."

Bell spoke up as she was trying to raise my hand to my medicine bag. I was not in a good position for her to do that. "That is why only Charles has been affected by headaches and no one else. Shamans from other cultures... that live half a world away. Eve, it must have been Lars time traveling that somehow caused his headaches and now Chastity. You're sure he will never leave the 7th century again?"

"I am positive of that. Now. We need to bring this poor man back to us. Okay, Chastity. Try that healing spell again. This time Mister Blue does need healing."

"I don't know, Mother, I don't want to hurt him again. I..."

"Dear, that is good to know. And to know you have good inside of you. Go ahead. He does need healing now."

Chastity reluctantly reached over and put her hand on my head and recited the same spell.

I blinked, opened my eyes, and sat up, leaning on my elbows. My headache was gone. I looked up at Chastity and saw tears streaming down her face.

She quickly removed her hand. "Are… are you… Mister Blue. Are you okay?"

"I am almost fine. I'm just weak. I need to do the rest myself. Chastity, you can watch. I'll even recite my personal healing spell out loud."

And I did. I grabbed my medicine bag and recited the spell. I once again saw Grandfather in my mind. As soon as I finished, I jumped up and gave Bell a strong hug.

Chastity had a questioning look on her face. "Mister Blue, I thought I saw someone hovering over you. Some old man in a black suit and top hat."

"You can see Grandfather? Chastity, that was the spirit of Peter Red Feather. My shaman grandfather. Incredible."

Everyone, Granny, Bell, Eve, and Grace, said the same thing. "Incredible."

When Chastity stood back up, Eve gave her a good loving hug. Grace came over to do the same. Chastity started to back away but decided not to. She reached out to her half-sister, and they hugged like good sisters should.

"Dear friends," Eve said. "We should be getting back to Saxmundham. Sven is there trying to run the pub all by himself and I'm sure he misses Grace."

"Mother?"

"Yes, Chastity."

"Will father… I mean Ian… will he be joining us?"

"No, dear, he won't. He loves his little museum in Dunwich. I plan to join him there, and I hope to help him find his artifacts that were stolen."

I remembered something. "Granny, have you looked in your satchel lately?"

"What are you talking about, Charles?" I smiled at

Granny, and she reached over and opened it. "Oh. That's what you meant. How did these get here? You?" She pointed at me.

"Nope. Tobias, I think. Bell and I noticed that there was only one item in here wrapped in your coated cheesecloth. These others are in plain cheesecloth. Different feel to them. Go ahead and open them."

Eve was looking over Granny's shoulder. "Yana, none of these are from Ian's collection. A couple of these are from the British Museum. But I believe these bracelet halves were stolen from the dig in 1939. I was there when these were found. Basil left these with Edith Pretty along with many of the findings. I don't think they ever went to the British Museum after the war. I wonder why? They are so unique."

"And so out of place," Bell said. "Just like when we saw the griffin... dragon ring. Yana, hold up those two pieces and join them together."

"Dear?"

"Please."

"Okay, dear, here goes."

"Now. Charles, come here and bring your ring close to it. I'll do it too."

Our rings began to glow, first very lightly, then a little stronger, but not as strong as when we time traveled. Small specks began to glow all around the bracelet. Bell pointed with her free hand. "See. There are pieces of amber embedded in this carved bracelet. And... Oh my gods and goddesses!"

The glowing made the bracelet mend itself. It was whole again.

"Could this be the original time piece? It looks like some of the amber pieces are missing. Are they on our rings:" I asked no one in particular. Bell, Granny, and Eve just shrugged as they kept staring at it. Bell and I stepped back, and the bracelet's glow diminished.

"Yana," Bell said. "If this was stolen by someone in this time who went back to 1939 and stole the pieces from Edith Pretty's house, we should go back there ourselves and return this."

"Bell, it won't be the same," I said. "It was in two pieces. It is now a single full bracelet, not what was found in Sutton Hoo back then. Right, Eve?"

"True. We'd have to break it in two again."

"Please do not do that."

Granny's little room at the inn was getting crowded even more. An older woman, not quite as old as Granny, appeared by the door. She was several inches taller than Granny, at least five foot four, and wore the type of outfit fishermen wear. Hooded yellow windbreaker and matching yellow rain pants. She had on black wellies, Wellington boots. She was attractive, and her blond hair did not have any grey in it.

"I am so sorry to barge in, but I have been watching you for a while."

"Watching us? How?" I asked.

"Easy. I have a crystal that shows me whatever I wish to see."

"Really?" Granny said. "I, too, have a crystal that used to work like that. Unfortunately, mine is cracked and doesn't work anymore. Uh… who are you?"

"I am so sorry. I forgot to introduce myself. My name is Haldis. Haldis Asulf."

"Asulf?" I questioned. "Any relation to Lars Asulf?"

"Why… yes. That is my… brother."

Chapter 21

Chastity walked up to her. "You… you're my aunt?"

"I beg your pardon?"

"I just found out from mother, here…" Chastity put her hand on Eve's arm. "…that Lars was my real father."

"Really? Well… that man did have a way with women. Ha. I should say he had his way with many women. You… probably had a dozen or more half brothers and sisters in the 7th century. Long, long gone now."

"I thought I understood from not only Lars, but from a young Ian and Tobias that you were murdered by Malcolm the Cruel."

"Oh, he thought so. He often called me a witch… well, I am. When I was… captured by Malcolm and in… brought to his village, he drugged and weakened me. He kept me in that state, so… he could take advantage of me. I gave birth to first Ian, then only ten months later, Tobias. While… uh, pregnant with Tobias, Malcolm was dallying with other women he and his men captured that year. He stopped drugging me. I strengthened again. After that Malcolm was never able to couple with me. Ha. I made sure he could not… well, perform anymore… with anyone. When his… my children were barely three and four he came at me with his short sword right in front of the children. To them, he killed me. In reality, I staged my death. I was much stronger and… was able to put a spell on Malcolm making him think he killed me. His… my boys thought he killed me. I knew as young men, Malcolm would train them as warriors, so I kept a remote watch on them. Well, I… Tobias followed more in Malcolm's footsteps than Ian. Ian was a romantic and fell for Malcolm's more recent conquest—you, Eve."

Grace had been quiet and standing aside while the conversations continued. She finally spoke. "Miss…"

"Haldis."

"If I understand this right, Chastity's father, your brother, Lars, makes you her aunt. My father, Ian, was one of your sons. So does that mean you are my… grandmother?"

"Huh? Uh…you are right." Haldis laughed.

Bell and I looked at each other and knew what we had to ask. I started. "Haldis, you are the… skipper of the Anglo Saxon? That two-masted sailboat?"

"Yes. Yes, I am. It is a ketch I was able to procure and convert in the 1920s."

"Convert?" Bell asked.

"For traveling to places and time. And… looking for special people… like you, Bell, to make the rings you both wear."

Both Bell and Granny were staring at Haldis. Granny spoke, "Ah! Maybe that is why you seem familiar to me. Bell? You too?" Bell didn't say anything and kept staring. Granny continued, "You came to my shop, the Mystic Eye, in San Francisco, back in 1961. You appeared out of the thick fog outside."

"Well… yes. The fog is my protection going to and from a place or time."

"But why did you bring the two bodies back? Thomas and his uncle, Garrett Stone?" I asked.

"I was… well, so distressed when I saw what Tobias had become. First, he became obsessed with you, Eve, then with the money he hoped to obtain selling all of Ian's and Henry's artifacts. He… uh… I knew Tobias had the cruelty in him like his father, Malcolm."

"Haldis, did you ever see any book, like a leather-bound notebook anywhere in your journeys?" Granny asked.

"No. I did not." She said looking away from us with a frown

Hope it's still hidden in Thomas's apartment, I thought. Then I asked, "What about Garrett?"

Haldis paused, then said, "After… uh, Tobias killed him, he tossed him over the cliff thinking the fall would mask the murder. He… I saw what he was doing, so I created a thick fog… so Tobias could not see where the body landed. I willed it into my rubber boat and then put him into my ketch." She paused again. "

"But why?" Bell asked. "Why take them both back to San Francisco?"

"I… was trying to stop Tobias. When he brought Henry… uh, Thomas Stone to his home, Tobias only did that to try to find some journal, the one you mentioned, that he had been looking for. Thomas was still alive but suffering from the spacial travel, both mentally and physically. I… invisibly followed Tobias and tried to… uh, use my powers remotely to calm Thomas down so he could drink some water, but he was, how do the young people say, freaking out. I was able to get him to drink some water, so I left." She paused again. "Tobias must have returned and strangled the weakened Thomas and I… uh, he magically rolled him up in a rug. I came back in solid form, oh, fifteen minutes later, to… check on Thomas and found his apartment torn up and the young man dead. Suffocated. Miss Blue… Yana, after Tobias later killed Garrett, he… went to your house thinking it was still Garrett's. He went there to again to look for the journal and any artifacts Henry might have given his brother. He was very disappointed it was not Garrett's anymore and left without damaging anything. I… am afraid I… he… uh, raided your refrigerator though."

"But why did you capture our friend Patrick?" I asked.

"Patrick? I know of no one named Patrick. And I did not capture anyone. Why do you ask?"

"Our friend lost a full day of his life. He came to check out your boat and thought he was only gone a couple of hours when he finally returned to his apartment. His clothes were ripped and dirty, and he was bruised like he was in a fight. He says he was on your boat. Oh, and his apartment was also torn up."

"No. Not me. Not on my boat. I… would not have… wait! Tobias again.! It had to be him. He must have taken your friend… from the dock right in front of my boat. He probably thought your friend was another who knew about the journal."

"What is so important about that journal?" I asked. "Why was Tobias searching for it?"

"Uh… Well, unfortunately, I have no idea. There may be some spells or some other sensitive sor… uh, witch or warlock information Tobias heard about somehow. Maybe through young Thomas's mind. Mortals… are easy to read. If Tobias couldn't find it in Thomas's home, I'm sure… his anger got the best of him, and he then killed the young man."

I noticed Bell had her eyes closed. We were still holding hands while listening to Haldis. I closed my eyes too, and saw what Bell was checking out in Haldis's mind. How could we read a witch's mind? Is she something other than a witch? We now both had the same feeling she was making up her stories.

And Haldis knew we were probing her mind. Her demeanor changed. She clenched her fists and her smile turned upside down.

"Damn! You two are in my mind! That cannot be! How..."

Bell answered. "I had to make sure what you were saying was true or not. It was not. You murdered our friend and his nephew, and I'm sure, the real Tobias."

"And you are not Haldis Asulf," I said. "You are not related to Lars Asulf. Tell us your real name."

"I AM HALDIS ASULF!" She yelled while coming toward us. "You two lie! You lie!"

She looked like she was about to pull something out of her coat pocket.

Before she could grab whatever she had in her pocket, Eve stepped up between Haldis and us and grabbed her by the hand and quickly raised it. Her ring finger was missing.

So that small finger and ring that Eve smashed belonged to Haldis. She must be a shape shifter. Has she been the 'evil' Tobias this whole time? Where is the real Tobias?

Haldis pulled away from Eve and pulled her left hand out of her pocket. In her grip was another dragon ring she had been hiding. Ian's stolen ring? It was glowing. Haldis was about to disappear. Bell and I both jumped at her, our rings glowing, and grabbed her. As all three of us disappeared, I heard Granny, Eve, and the others yelling "NO!"

Chapter 22

The light from three rings was so bright, and the thunder from them so loud all of us were blinded and deafened.

I used my medicine bag to quickly help me and Bell, but when we were able to see and hear again, Haldis was nowhere around. She must have gone somewhere else using her second ring when Bell and I lost our grip on her.

"Bell. We lost her."

"Maybe in this time. See where we are? It's dark. But there's lights flashing over there."

"Holy… Sutton Hoo! There's the ship re-buried to hide and protect it. Wait. We're back in the 1940s again. I thought my ears were still ringing from the thunder. Those are bombs going off along the coast down there." I pointed south. "We're back here with the war going on. The blitz."

"I think we're safe here for now. If I remember right, this area was never bombed during the war. This war. There are no military bases around here. The only building is Edith Pretty's house over there."

"So, Bell, where do you think Haldis went?"

"I'm sure she's back in her era, getting ready to change

time to her advantage."

"Shall we?"

"Yes. But by all the gods and goddesses, I hope this will be over soon. I really hate this time traveling!"

"Ditto."

We held hands and put our rings close to each other while thinking of 7th century, Malcolm's village. Another bright flash and clap of thunder.

As soon as our eyes and ears adjusted, I recognized the location we appeared at. It was the same place we came to before. And, once more, two teenage boys were trotting toward us. Ian and Tobias. Tobias spoke telepathically.

"You are back? Did we not tell you before how dangerous it is here for you? You should leave quickly!"

"Brother, be content. They must be here for a reason."

"We are," I answered. *"We are trying to find a black witch who came from this time who has murdered people in our time. She called herself Haldis."*

"Our aunt?" They both said.

"Aunt? Is she your father's sister?" Bell asked.

Tobias answered. *"Yes. And we try to stay away from her. She is a warrior witch, as cruel, or maybe worse than father. Our aunt is the one who put a spell on father to kill mother. She is still trying to sway the two of us to her style of witchcraft. We just want to live normal lives. We do not want to be warriors... or warlocks."*

"I think you will have the lives you want... someday," I said out loud knowing they couldn't understand the language. They looked at me oddly. I then asked, *"Do you know where Haldis is right now?"*

Ian answered. *"She told everyone she just returned from*

battle. I overheard her tell father. She showed him her severed finger saying the warrior who cut it off was now dead."

"That's not true. I know how that happened. Is she with your father now?" I asked.

"No. She has her own place. Right over that hill." Ian pointed.

Bell had a question. "If Haldis and your father are brother and sister, why isn't your father a warlock like you two? You've always told us your father called himself a shaman, but you said he isn't. Is that true?"

Ian answered. "Father is… well, not very bright. If he has any powers at all, he would not know what to do with them. Haldis, on the other hand, is smart, which makes her dangerous. She has put a spell on father to make him kill witches she points out, so she has no competition. Also, it is she who plans father's battles, conquests, and murders."

"Ian, Tobias, we must go and confront Haldis. She knows about…"

Bell put her finger up to my mouth to shush me. She spoke out loud so the others couldn't understand us. "Charles. Don't mention anything to them that could change history. No one here knows about the buried ship and the ring that's in it. They can't know about that. We must keep Haldis from getting that other ring, Eve's ring, from the boat burial."

Both Ian and Tobias looked worried. "Haldis is too powerful," Tobias said. Ian then added, "We are not. Are you? Confronting her could be your death."

"She has killed too many, in your time and in ours," Bell told them. "She will continue to do the same, and more, unless we can stop her."

"We have been up against adversaries as powerful as her," I said. "Besides, we can't die here in your time. That really would change history."

"But will killing her change history?" Ian asked me.

"It shouldn't. She is of your time, and we must prevent her from escaping to the future ever again. Now. Over that hill you say."

As we stealthily headed up the hill, the two young teenagers ran off the other direction to their own home.

When we reached the top of the hill, we laid down on the leaf-covered ground and looked down at a small wattle and daub house with a thatched roof. It looked awfully plain. For a warrior witch I expected something more castle like.

"That's Haldis's home?" I questioned, whispering in Bell's ear.

"Something's not right," Bell commented. "Look. Someone's coming."

An old woman came around the house from the back with an armful of wool and went in the short, narrow front door, which was only an opening covered with cloth.

"Okay. This is the direction Ian and Tobias pointed, isn't it?" I questioned.

"Yes, Charles. It is." Bell closed her eyes then opened them. "I'm really getting the feeling Haldis is faking this. That old woman might have been her shape shifting again."

"So, why don't we appear behind the hill over there and see if the house looks different from the back side."

"I have a better idea, lover. Remember how Eve could enter like a phantom to check out a location before traveling there in person? You wanted to try that. I think now is the time. We can… well, look inside the house to see what we're dealing with."

"Uh… you know, maybe we should test it before we look in the house. Make sure we can do it."

"Okay but be sure to think positive about it. Let's appear on the hill behind the house and see what we can see."

We turned over on our backs and held hands, closed our eyes, then put our rings close to each other.

I could see the back of the house on the inside of my eyelids. I didn't see Bell though. The back of the house did look different than the front. In fact, the back wall was stone, and quite large, like a fortress, right down to a couple of narrow arrow slits through the thick rock near the top.

Okay. That proves that what we first saw in front was not real. I opened my eyes and looked over at Bell. Her eyes were also open.

"Well. That was interesting," I said. "I didn't see you though."

"I was there. I didn't see you either. Maybe we can't see each other's ghostly figures."

"You did see the castle?"

"Yes. And I think I saw movement up top on the battlements. I'd swear I saw a man looking down on us. It could be one of Haldis's guards."

"I missed that. Crud. Hey! I just remembered. We saw Eve's ghostly image when she was by Ian. If a guard saw us and reported it to Haldis, our goal could be compromised. She might already know we are close by and what we're up to."

"We have to change our plan, lover, and think this out."

We kept watching the front of her dwelling, which still looked like an old wattle and daub shack. However…

"Bell. Did you see that?"

"Yes, I did. That shack turned into a castle for a split second then back again. Haldis must be up to something. Maybe she lost concentration on her visual spell."

And a few seconds later we heard the sound of leaves crunching under someone's feet and coming up behind us.

We quickly turned around.

"Tobias?" we both said. "What…"

Then we took a better look. This was an older looking Tobias, and he was increasing his speed toward us and pulled a war ax from behind him. No, it was not him. Haldis had again shape shifted to look like Tobias, and now turned back into herself.

She started to run straight at me with her ax raised and ready to strike. She was almost upon me when Bell jumped between us. Bell crossed her arms and stared into Haldis's eyes.

The ax swung hard like Haldis planned to sever Bell's head from her shoulders. It was close, but instead of hitting Bell, the blade seemed to hit a solid wall and bounced back, surprising Haldis. The ax flew out of her hand and landed more than twenty feet behind her.

She quickly recovered and pulled a short sword from its sheath on her side. Her face changed from anger to madness. She let out a loud, shrill war cry as she charged at us again. It was a frightening sound.

Bell still stood her ground. I stood beside her. Both our arms were crossed, and we stared at Haldis's eyes.

Haldis was attempting to stab at me with all the strength she had, and her sword again hit a solid invisible wall. She yelled something in the ancient language of the time and stabbed at me again. Somehow, her words countered my spell, and her sword pierced through to me. It got deflected enough by my spell that her sword went into and through my shoulder, knocking me down. I was sure she was going to finish me off.

Except for one thing. Bell.

When she saw me fall with the sword in me, her anger

rose. Haldis jerked her sword from my shoulder and came at Bell. At the same time, Bell came at Haldis. They were almost face to face. Bell's ring was glowing intensely. She pointed the light at Haldis. Lightning, along with a loud clap of thunder, came out of it, striking the second ring Haldis now wore, causing her to pause in wonder. Bell raised her hand and somehow the war ax leapt into it.

Bell let out a terrifying scream, like Haldis's war cry, as she swung it.

A head bounced down the hillside and became lodged in a bush, its surprised looking wide eyes staring up to the sky.

Within seconds, Haldis's body and head turned to dust. Only her ring remained.

Bell swung the ax again and crushed the ring. It flashed once then died, also turning to dust. She then dropped the ax and ran to me. I had passed out in a pool of my blood.

Time stopped for both of us.

Bell leaned back and stared. Grandfather, Peter Red Feather, appeared sitting next to me with his hand on my wound. His other hand was on my medicine bag. He looked up at Bell and motioned for her to sit down on the other side of me and put her hand over his on my wound and her other hand over the medicine bag. I awoke and cried out in pain.

Chapter 23

I was in intense pain. With both Bell and Grandfather working in tandem, the pain lessened enough so I was able to grit my teeth and hold my medicine bag by myself and mumble the Ohlone healing spell. The bleeding stopped, and the wound closed. My broken shoulder bones were still healing, making me wince.

I opened my eyes and was now able to see the two of them. Grandfather in his ghostly form, and a tearful Bell holding onto me like she didn't want to let go. I smiled at her then noticed she was splattered in Haldis's blood and probably some of mine when she hugged me.

I felt Grandfather remove his hand from my shoulder. He smiled at me. I mouthed "thank you", then he disappeared.

Time started again.

"Oh… my… wonderful dear lover," Bell said through sobs. "I'm so happy you are alive. I really thought Haldis killed you. From where I was standing it looked like her sword went through your chest."

"Oh Bell. I love you. I was surprised Haldis was able to counter our blocking. Mine was still working a little and her sword was blocked enough to send it through my shoulder instead of into my heart. Uh… how did you…"

"Dispatch Haldis?"

"Yeah. When I got hit, I thought she had the upper hand. What did you do?"

"Lover, I'll tell you later. Why don't we head back to our time in Dunwich so we can shower… together… so we can scrub off all this… uh… red stuff.

With Bell still holding onto me, we pictured our destination as our rings glowed.

The long journey back to our time again created a very bright flash and clap of thunder. When our eyes cleared and our hearing returned, we saw we were back in our room at the Ship Inn and Pub.

With all the blood caked on us, we wanted to get cleaned up before meeting up with Granny and Ian. Bell mentally scanned outside our door and said it was clear to head to the bathroom at the end of the hall.

Forty minutes later we were dressed in clean clothes and looked in Granny's room. She was not there. We headed downstairs.

And there was Granny sitting in a wooden booth by the front window. However, she was not sitting with Ian. Across from her was…

"Garrett!" Bell and I both exclaimed.

"Huh? What?" Garrett questioned. "You look surprised to see me."

Bell and I looked at each other and suddenly realized we had changed history. Or… did we replace the history that Haldis had changed with the real thing? We'd have to talk about that later.

Granny looked at us and I could see she understood fully.

She winked and said, "Did you kids have a nice trip?

"Uh… yes, Granny, we had an… exciting time."

"You must tell me about it later. Oh, and Ian wanted to see you when you returned. He's next door at his museum."

If history is as it should be… "Before Bell and I head over there… uh… Garrett. How is your brother, Henry?"

"He's doing much better. I made sure his debts were taken care of. I think his ordeal with his bookie's thugs cured him of his gambling."

I started to ask Garrett about his nephew, Thomas, but thought better of it. If Henry Stone is still alive, then Thomas never made it to England. In this history, we shouldn't know who Thomas is.

Bell and I looked at each other again and shrugged. We said our goodbyes and headed to the museum.

We climbed the thirteen steps to the front door, which was open, and walked in. Well, the museum looked the same. Ian was standing over a display case polishing the glass top. He turned to us and smiled. Eve came in through the door to Ian's bedroom and also smiled at us.

"Ian. Eve. So good to see you again," I said.

"You act like you have not seen us a while," Eve said.

"And I have something to talk to you two about." Ian said. "But it will have to wait until…. Ah. I hear him driving up now."

A familiar sounding car. I thought. "Bell? Could it be?"

Before she could answer, a figure came in the front door.

"Tobias!"

"Hi you two. Okay Ian, I'm here. Let's all go into your secret room and talk. Eve can watch the front if any customers come in."

Ian touched the bookcase, and it slid aside. The four of us

entered the room and the bookcase closed.

Ian's cabinets were still there. The glass was still there. And I was sure the artifacts were still hidden behind the glass.

Ian began. "Tobias and I have talked it over and we wanted to thank both of you for all you have done for us. We've known who you are for… how long has it been brother? Some 1400 years?"

Tobias continued. "We were mere children still a few years away from full manhood when you appeared to us. With our home back then so dysfunctional, with father's stupidity and our aunt's black witch cruelty, the two of us tried to stay away and in the forest as much as we could. I remember you coming twice to that time and place. When you killed our wicked aunt, our whole village celebrated thinking Ian and I did it. With father out from under Haldis's spells, he now took it upon himself to resume his own cruelty. He really did become Malcolm the Cruel. It was then he began raiding more and brought back a very young Eve as his next conquest. I think the rest you know."

"But, as I am sure you know, this information cannot go beyond this room," Ian said. Then chuckled. "Well, no one would believe it anyway."

Both Ian and Tobias shook my hand and Bell gave them both hugs.

The bookcase opened. Bell and I left and went back to the pub and sat down with Granny and Garrett.

Granny spoke. "Dear ones, I think it's about time for us to go home." She laughed. "Heh. This time… let's take a plane."

Epilogue

Bell and I had been home for a week. We were finally over our jet lag, so we invited Patrick over for dinner. We were curious how history had changed in San Francisco.

Before dinner, we sat around the living room sipping a nice cabernet.

"So, Patrick," I began. "We haven't talked for a while. How have you been?"

"Good. The big news is that I finally got my PI license. And, I already have a case."

"That's really neat," Bell said. "What's the case?"

"Sorry, but I can't really talk about it. Not until it's over anyway. All I can say is I'm working with Castillo again."

"Ah. And how is Castillo?" I asked.

"He's a happy camper. He got promoted to captain while you were gone. He has the job I used to have in homicide."

We spent the rest of the evening catching up and telling Patrick about the places we visited. We didn't mention anything about our time traveling. No need to say anything to him about changing history.

The following day Bell and I were curious about another thing. How is Thomas Stone and is Garrett's notebook there?

We picked up Granny and drove to Cow Hollow. I found a parking place only a half block from the apartment building. It was an easy level walk, and Granny didn't need any of my medicine bag help.

Like before, as we were checking the names on the list of tenants, Mac came out to greet us and introduced himself again. And again, he seemed smitten by Granny. Well, in that respect, history is repeating itself. Now, what about Thomas?

"It's good to meet you, Mac," I said. "We came to talk to Thomas Stone. His uncle, Garrett Stone, wanted us to pick up a book of his that he was giving to my grandmother here. I think he called you."

I was assuming this part of history would repeat too. Hopefully, Thomas's death wasn't part of it.

"Oh yes. Garrett. He did call Thomas and said you would be stopping by. Thomas sometimes works on Saturdays, but I saw him earlier when he went to the store. Nice boy. He picks up a few things for me too. Let me take you upstairs. We can take the elevator miss… uh, Yana."

It was a small elevator, similar to the one in Patrick's building. Bell and I said we'd take the stairs. Mac told us Thomas's apartment number. He didn't have to, Bell and I remembered from before.

The elevator arrived the same time Bell and I got up the stairs. Mac knocked on Thomas's door.

I didn't hear anything and began to worry something happened to Thomas like before.

Bell heard my thoughts and spoke to me telepathically. *"Don't worry, lover, I sense movement."*

And the door opened. A tall gangly man stood there smiling. Mac introduced us.

"So nice to meet you all. My uncle Garrett told me you were coming. Can I get you anything? No? Okay. Let me get uncle's notebook for you."

With all hoopla surrounding Haldis's search for Garrett's book, I was curious where it was hidden. Or not hidden.

Thomas pulled a leather-bound journal from a small bookshelf next to his easy chair and handed it to Granny. It had a hasp and lock keeping it shut. How was that missed when this apartment was overturned before? Unless Garrett only allowed his nephew to be able to see it. With both Thomas and Garrett dead in the alternate history, Garrett's journal disappeared. Now both alive, the journal existed and was in Granny's hands.

We talked to Thomas for a few minutes more letting him know how his grandfather and uncle in England were doing. He told us he wished he could go to England someday and visit them.

We took Granny back to her house and she invited us in. She wanted us all together when she opened Garrett's notebook. She first handed it to Bell, who mumbled a couple of words making the lock drop off the leather cover. She handed it back to Granny.

"Well, children, let's see why this book is so important."

Granny opened it to the first page.

"Oh, my gods and goddesses!"

"What? What?" Bell and I both said trying to glance at what Granny was reading. We couldn't see it.

Granny didn't say anything. She kept reading and turning pages. After several pages she took a deep breath and set the book down, closed, on her lap. She looked up at us. She had tears in her eyes.

"Children. This was written before history changed.

Garrett says he knew about Haldis. He knew she would kill him in Dunwich. This journal is his last will and testament… if he really died."

"But Garrett is alive," Bell said. "He's alive in this time and place."

"Yes, he is, thank the gods and goddesses. And Garrett wrote why Haldis wanted his journal. He tells how Haldis wanted Henry Stone's house any way she could. Evidently, most of the rock his house was made of came from Haldis's castle when it collapsed around the 12th century. The rock has some kind of magic embedded in it that Haldis needed for her spells. She was going to live there and reestablish her reign of terror in the 20th century, first killing all those with powers who might be a threat to her… like Tobias and Ian, who she knew from the 7th century. Also, she needed to find and destroy this journal."

"I'm glad everyone is alive. Granny, I almost died at Haldis's hand back then. Her sword went all the way through my shoulder. If not for Bell's swift move, the outcome might have been totally different."

"Dear Charles. You didn't tell me that. You are okay, aren't you?"

"Grandfather, along with Bell, got me started healing. Then I was able to use my medicine bag to complete it. The scars remain though. They'll always remind me of another time and place."

"Now, children, we must destroy this journal. Yes, Garrett told me he wanted it destroyed. It is of a history that no longer exists. Come. Time to use the fireplace. Charles, please get a couple pieces of firewood from the garage."

I retrieved two small logs and put them on the grate, on top of the book Granny placed there. Granny then did something I remember our wizard friend Dean had done. She clapped her hands and the logs ignited fully. I was surprised. Another thing Granny never told me she could do. More secrets.

The journal burned up along with the logs. Granny sifted the ashes to make sure it was completely gone. It was.

Several hours later, Bell and I were back in our loft in our Victorian. It had been a long day and we both wanted to get some rest. We undressed for bed.

"Uh… Charles, I thought you said your scars remained."

"Yeah. They've been there since we came back from the 7th century." I touched my shoulder when I said that. "Hey! It's gone."

"Go look in the mirror."

I did. "Holy… Bell they are gone, like I was never stabbed."

"History has changed, lover. Well, except for one thing…"

She grabbed my hand and pulled me to the bed. We made love over and over again until we both fell asleep hours later, exhausted.

The historical information on Dunwich, Saxmundham, and the dig at Sutton Hoo are all true. Early in the 21st century, my wife and I visited a friend in Saxmundham. The inn we stayed in, with its attached pub was my inspiration for Tobias's establishment.

While staying in Saxmundham, our English friend drove us around to explore the several castles that still exist in East Anglia. One was tall and had a much smaller footprint on the land than all the others we visited. All you could see from the outside were rows of arrow slits. I thought of this castle when writing about Haldis's.

My description and location of Henry Stone's old house was a figment of my imagination. However, we found out that some of the old stone houses we saw, as well as stone walls in the countryside were built using material repurposed from other castle ruins and old buildings around the area.

We also visited Dunwich and learned about the interesting history of the town. The ruins of Greyfriars

Monastery was a short walk from there. Most of the graves in Greyfriars Woods have actually fallen into the sea. Over hundreds of years, bones would occasionally appear sticking out of the cliff before falling into the sea.

In Dunwich, the Ship Inn is a real establishment. When we visited it nearly twenty years ago, it was the local pub and inn. Now it appears to be a more high-end restaurant with modern rooms in other buildings, including one next door to the pub that I used as Ian's museum.

Four of the characters I mention at the Sutton Hoo digs are real: Basil Brown, Edith Pretty and her son Robert, and Charles Phillips. All the other characters at the dig are fictitious as were all the characters and stories from ancient Sutton Hoo.

Charles Blue, Bell, and Granny will return in

A Warlock in Provence.